NAT
SWITCH

11+

NATHAN'S SWITCH

PAT MOON

ORCHARD BOOKS

F15y

Lines quoted from "Another Brick
in the Wall (Part 2)" by Roger
Waters © 1979 are reproduced by
permission of Pink Floyd Music
Publishers Limited.

ORCHARD BOOKS
96 Leonard Street, London EC2A 4RH
Orchard Books Australia
14 Mars Road, Lane Cove, NSW 2066
ISBN 1 85213 902 1 hardback
ISBN 1 85213 855 6 paperback
First published in Great Britain 1995
Text © Pat Moon 1995
A CIP catalogue record for this book is
available from the British Library.
Printed in Great Britain

*With thanks
to Nathan B., for his name and anything
else I have wittingly or unwittingly borrowed,
also to
Jane Wight, for all I needed to know
about bricks*

Also by Pat Moon

Double Image
The Spying Game

1
A Brick in the Wall

Nathan was halfway down Albert Road, practising his limp, when he remembered.

It's Dad's tonight, isn't it? Not Mum's.

He executed a perfect one hundred and eighty degree turn on his right foot, forgetting for the moment his limp, and headed back towards his old house where Dad lived: Bryjan, 23 Oaklands Road.

How'd I forget that? Made the arrangements myself, didn't I? Had to – seeing as Mum isn't talking to Dad.

"I can't face it, Nathe," Mum had said. "We'll only end up rowing again. It just makes things worse. You talk to him, Nathe."

"She's got to go somewhere tomorrow, something to do with work, I think," Nathan had explained to Dad over the phone from Mum's. "She won't be back till late. She says I'll have to come to you after school tomorrow – and can I stay the night?"

"Too busy to pick up the phone herself, is she?" Dad had said in his extra patient voice. "Her usual last-minute arrangements."

Nathan had counted the seconds, waiting for Dad's long sigh. One, two, three . . . It came right on cue.

"All right, Nathan. You know you can rely on me. See

you tomorrow then. And don't forget your key this time. We don't want another police enquiry regarding the sighting of a red-haired youth making a forced entry, do we, Nathan?"

As he backtracked down Albert Road, the picture of Mum's suitcases standing in the hallway floated into his head. He tried erasing it by superimposing a large bowl of toffee crunch ice-cream, topped with sliced banana, walnuts, cherries, maple syrup, a chocolate flake and fudge sauce. It didn't work. Instead, a picture of Mum and Dad playing tug of war with a cardboard box nudged its way in.

The whole event replayed itself in his head. It was the day he'd been taken sick at school. Mrs Grant, the school secretary, had rung Brindles where Mum worked, but she wasn't there; taken the day off, they said. And no one was answering the phone at home either. He'd sat outside the school office, crouched over a red bucket, listening to it all. In the end Mrs Grant had to ring Dad at Riley's Plastics. He wasn't pleased.

"What's your Mum playing at? She didn't say anything to me about taking a day off work."

Nathan hadn't answered. He'd been slumped across the back seat of Dad's car, fully occupied with being sick into the plastic bag Mrs Grant had given him.

They saw the two suitcases as soon as Dad pushed the front door open. And Mum, coming down the stairs with the box in her arms. She'd looked at them like a burglar might look caught red-handed with the TV set. Then she'd looked at Nathan and started to say something, when Dad had erupted. Nathan had never seen Dad like that before. Mum was usually the explosive one.

So he'd sat on the stairs, clasping his sick bag, watching them. Dad holding on to the box, demanding to know what was going on and Mum tugging the other end, not saying a word, as if suddenly her lips had become superglued together. Then suddenly she'd let go, everything spilling onto the floor: shoes, hairdryer, hot-water bottle . . .

Nathan could remember staring down at the green hot-water bottle and trying to work out its significance. And then Dad trying to stop her and Mum wrenching herself free. Dad, Mr Calm, Mr Let's-not-get-hysterical-shall-we? had gone volcanic. And when that hadn't worked he'd started rushing around the house labelling everything that was his with sticky Post-it notes. His record collection, the chess table that had taken all those weekends to make . . .

The house had looked as if a plague of yellow butterflies had invaded. It was like some crazy dream. He wouldn't have been surprised if Dad had suddenly set to with his new cordless screwdriver to remove the BRYJAN nameplate from the front gate, neatly slice it through with his Black and Decker variable-speed saw and stick a label on the BRY half.

But he hadn't, had he? thought Nathan, kicking a can into the gutter. As far as Dad was concerned, it was Bryan and Janice for ever. "She'll come to her senses, Nathan. You'll see. Just give her time to calm down. Act first, think later – that's your mother."

As it turned out, Mum had taken hardly anything at all.

Not even him. He tried not to think about that horrible day. It was as if he hadn't been there, the way they'd carried on. He'd felt invisible. Like this morning at Mum's, for instance. Had she noticed his limp? How he'd had to drag his leg painfully behind him to fetch the Cocopops? How reaching for the marmalade had caused him to wince? How he'd had to lean heavily on the chair as he made his way to the door? Had she enquired what ailed him? No. Just, "For goodness sakes, Nathan! Get a move on! You're going to make me miss my train!" And last time he'd stayed at Dad's there was no milk for his Cocopops. No Cocopops come to that.

Oh, Dad noticed him all right when a policeman greeted him on his return from work and asked him to confirm that he was not some mindless vandal observed behaving suspiciously in the vicinity of 23 Oaklands Road, but his son, Nathan Beazer, sometime resident of said address, who'd forgotten his key. And Mum had certainly noticed him when he'd accidentally used her new magazine in his papier-mâché mountain for geography homework on contour lines.

Hey – and why isn't *my* name on the front gate? It could have been added on when I made my entry into the world twelve and one twelfth years ago? There's room. If you squeeze the letters together a bit.

The thought brought Nathan to a second sudden halt, outside the Fresh 'n' Fruity Greengrocery.

"BRYJANATHE!" he proclaimed out loud, causing a woman browsing over the broccoli to turn and stare.

4

"You're talking to yourself again, Nathe," he told himself. "I have to," he answered. "I'm the only one who listens to me." The woman hurried into the shop.

BRYJANATHE. It's neat. Hang on. How about BRY-NATHE-JAN? Because that's where I am. Stuck in the middle. No. Not stuck. On the move. Shuttling between them, from one to the other, like that little ball in a pinball machine. And there's Nan's sometimes. Someone pulls a lever and – *doyng!* – off I go. Mum-Dad-Mum-Nan-Dad-Mum-Dad.

Nathan turned into Bakery Lane, staggering from side to side, ricocheting from imaginary obstacles. *Doyng! Doyng! Doyng-doyng-doyng!* He crashed backwards into a fence. Something rattled. It sounded like a pinball.

That's very good, Nathe. You did that without moving your lips.

As he hoisted up his backpack, the ball rattled again. He remembered now: it was the aerosol can of black paint he'd borrowed from Dad's shed. He'd taken it in for art this afternoon. They were making masks. His was nearly finished. He'd planned to paint it today and add the final touches. He'd called it "Death Stalks the Unwary". It was brilliant, even if he did say so himself. He'd taken in the paint, some of Mum's red nail varnish, a pair of joke eyes on springs, and some bones that Nan had saved for him from her "Entertaining with Chicken" class at the Over Sixties. All for nothing. Mr Jelly, their art teacher, was off sick, the art room was out of use because of the leaking roof, and Mrs Someone-or-other, the supply teacher, had trailed them round school for twenty minutes before finding an empty room in the mobiles. She'd handed out pencils and paper, grabbed a pathetic-looking spider plant from the radiator shelf and instructed them to draw it.

The afternoon would have been a complete waste of time if Nathan hadn't been suddenly inspired and turned his picture into "The Revenge of the Spider Plants from the Planet Zarpong". He'd been quite sorry when the bell had gone.

Nathan ambled slowly down the narrow lane.

No hurry. Dad won't be home till a quarter to six, at the earliest.

On the left of the lane ran a line of shabby fences and the backs of shops and houses. On the right, behind a long brick wall stood the old church hall and bakery. Both were boarded up. A large red and white sign ordered:

DANGER – KEEP OUT!

Nathan studied the graffiti.

ELVIS WAS HERE.

NO I WASN'T.

Kerry still loved Paul. Gary was a gorilla. Jesus saved with the Woolwich.

This place needs something new.

Nathan chose a suitable stretch of old wall, lowered his backpack and lifted out the can of paint.

Rule number one, Nathan. Always read the instructions first. That's what Dad says, isn't it?

He peered at the small print on the back of the can.

6

> Thoroughly clean area to be
> painted. Sand down with coarse,
> medium and then fine abrasive
> paper. Mask to prevent
> overspray. Prime bare areas
> with . . .

Stuff that. He read on.

> SHAKE CAN VIGOROUSLY FOR TWO
> MINUTES AND SPRAY 10″ FROM SURFACE.

That's more like it.

The ball rattled reassuringly as he shook.

What am I going to write, then?

BEWARE THE FEARLESS FOUR lit up in neon in his head.

What switched that on? That was yonks ago, when me and Gav and Sime and Nick were in the Juniors. Meetings in Nick's old shed, swearing oaths and printing secret badges with Gav's John Bull printing set. Till Nick's brother kicked the door in, that is – *and* swiped the ink pad. Oh yeah, and he had to go on about how "fearless" was spelt wrong and how we could easily change it to "The Feeble Four". Only not so politely as that. Gav stopped coming soon after, said he wasn't going to play if people kicked doors in instead of using the proper password. And what about his inkpad? And Sime's mum said she'd knock his block off if he came home with ink on his tracksuit again. You couldn't be fearless with Sime's mum. Then Nick moved away. Only me left. The Fearless One.

Oh well, have to be UP WITH LIVERPOOL. Can't think of anything else.

Checking the lane was clear, he gave the can a final rattle, held it up to spray and . . .

That brick's got a definite hint of – *magenta*, that's the word. Magenta, reddish-purple. And there's russet and rust and . . .

Colour names exploded from his memory banks. Aubergine and amber. Caramel and cinnabar. Ruby and claret. Lichen and lime. Vermilion and fuchsia.

Thank you, Miss King. Yeah, Miss King. My favourite teacher in the top Infants. Took us all out one day, showed us a wall just like this, made us notice all the different colours. Painted our own bricks, mixing colours and dabbing them on to paper brick shapes with sponges. Built a whole wall with them – it was excellent. And wasn't it Miss King who said my hair *wasn't* ginger? It was Titian!

Big mistake, that. They called me Tissue-head for weeks in the playground.

She said my painted brick was one of the best she'd seen. "I'm going to stick it right here in the middle where everyone will see it," she said.

Nathan smiled with smug pleasure just thinking about it. He still had it somewhere. Probably in his room at home.

Delete "home". Insert "Dad's". I'll dig it out tonight. I can use it to cheer myself up when the need arises.

8

Nathan stood there reliving his brick and the wall. He found himself doing this a lot lately. Thinking back. To when Sunday was Mum making Yorkshire pudding in the kitchen and Dad drilling or sawing or hammering somewhere. To the adventures of the Fearless Four. To when you got three gold stars for painting a brick.

Unlike yesterday when I'm made to stand up and explain why there's a minuscule piece of toast and Marmite, barely visible to the human eye, stuck to my diagram of an isosceles triangle. It's not my fault, is it, if the only place to do homework at Mum's is that shelf she calls a breakfast bar?

He stared at the wall.

OK, wall. You win. I'll let you off this time.

Shuffling footsteps brought him abruptly back to the present. An old man was coming towards him, trailing a shopping basket on wheels. Nathan slipped the can inside his jacket, picked up his bag and ambled slowly on, allowing the old man to overtake him. He stopped before a pair of peeling and tilting padlocked garage doors, took out his can, shook it and quickly sprayed.

UP WITH LIVER

He shook the can again and pressed the button. Only a hiss of gas. The paint had run out. Up with liver?

Nothing was going right today.

Nothing was going right this year.

A noise behind him made him turn. Then a voice.

"Oi! You!"

A very large man was leaning out of a window above the betting shop, shaking a fist at him.

"... if I get my 'ands on you, you won't 'ave no liver. Cos I'm gonna personally remove it and shove it ..."

The Fearless One grabbed his bag and legged it round the corner as fast as he could.

It was there that he found the switch.

2
~
The Switch
~

The object that first caught Nathan's eye as he turned the corner was the gigantic plastic blue tube. It writhed like a monstrous caterpillar from the top-floor window of an old building that was being gutted further along the road. He ambled curiously towards the large, yellow skip beneath it.

Oh yeah! Excellent! A skip.

A board announced:

GLEBE HOUSE COURT
PRESTIGIOUS DEVELOPMENT
OF 1–3 BEDROOM APARTMENTS

He had to have a quick look at least. It was amazing what other people threw away, he thought, remembering the stuffed stoat he'd found in a skip last year. It only had one leg missing. One day he might strike really lucky, like Sime's brother who'd found an old telephone and sold it to the bric-à-brac shop for £15.

Nathan reached up, grasped the edge of the skip, heaved himself up and peered in. Yuk. A stained mattress, pieces of splintered wood and some bits of rotting carpet, all covered in rubble and drink cans. Legs dangling, he steadied himself with one hand, grabbed a piece of wood with the other, pushed the carpet to one side and poked at the rubbish beneath.

11

Phfaw! Something – or someone – must have died in here.

The mattress looked old enough to be harbouring plague germs. He had a sudden vision of himself staggering home, covered in pulsating black boils, and Mum saying, "Get a move on, Nathan ..."

He turned his head, took a gulp of fresh air and, holding his breath, probed once more into the depths. Something glimmered. Balancing precariously like a seesaw, he stretched, grabbed and pulled. A brass buckle attached to a leather strap emerged. But whatever was attached to the other end was firmly stuck. He levered beneath it with the wood, tugged, levered, tugged, levered, tugged ... Suddenly something shot forward into his arms, sending him toppling backwards onto the path. His head filled with shattering sounds.

"Blooming Henry," mumbled Nathan. White-faced, he stared up from the path where he lay propped by his bulging backpack. For the sounds were not, as he first suspected, his bones breaking, but a torrent of razor-edged spears of glass shooting from the blue tube into the skip. He stood up and, from a cautious distance, stared in shocked silence. Shards of glass quivered like daggers from the mattress and carpet, where only seconds before he had been rummaging.

He noticed he was clasping something to his chest. A small wooden box with a leather strap and a brass buckle. Sounds from above made him look up. Workmen were knocking out a window. He'd had enough for one day. He hoisted the strap over his shoulder and made his way Bryjan-wards.

Death had stalked. But Nathan the Unwary had somehow survived.

Nathan pressed his nose hopelessly against the double glazing of Dad's Alaska All-Weather front porch. After an exhaustive search of pockets, coat lining and backpack he'd come to the unwelcome conclusion that he'd left his key in his other jacket. Again. He looked at his watch. Ten past four. Over an hour and a half till Dad got home. A cold wind blew up his trouser legs as the first few drops of rain splattered onto the glass. He headed for the carport and squatted on his backpack.

Lifting the wooden box onto his knee, he examined it from all sides. It was roughly the size of a thick book, made from dark wood, shiny but scratched. A lid was fastened by four tarnished brass clasps, two at the front and two at the back. Nathan released the clasps, lifted off the shallow lid and peered inside. There was a large brass dial at the top and below it a row of four smaller brass dials, each with a pointer hand, gleaming in the dull light. Each hand pointed upwards to the word OFF written in black ink on the wood. The dials were marked off at intervals and numbered with black ink around their rims. Beneath the dials were shadows of more writing which, in the gloom, he couldn't quite make out. A large brass button, like a doorbell, was screwed into the bottom right corner. Nathan stabbed at it with a finger. Not a sound. In the top left corner was a

13

small brass switch. The leather strap at each side divided into four brass chains that connected to the four corners of the box. He stood up and looped the strap over his head. The box hung just below waist level, like an usherette's ice-cream tray.

"Mmmm," hummed Nathan with growing curiosity.

He turned the hands on one of the dials and pressed the brass button. Nothing. He flicked the brass switch into the down position and pressed the button again. Still nothing. He tried various permutations with dials on and off and the switch up or down, stabbing the button at intervals. He was just becoming bored with it when a sudden humming made him jump and his finger shot off the button. Immediately the humming ceased. But the hum hadn't come from the box. It had come from inside *him*. His head was still buzzing.

He sat down and had a think. *Always read the instructions first, Nathan*, Dad's voice reminded him. He picked up the lid. Ah! What's this? Some more writing inside.

He read the careful, sloping letters:

McKay's Automatic Time Dial Apparatus
(Prototype 4)
Hamish McKay, B.Sc., A.R.C.S, A.R.I.C., D.I.C.
(Inventor)

Nathan slapped his forehead as realisation hit him.

It's some sort of time switch, isn't it? Dad has them all over the place: switching the central heating on and off, bringing on the washing machine for off-peak electricity in

14

the middle of the night, all part of his Energy Saving Drive. They don't look like this, but they've got dials and markings and numbers. This is probably one of the first ever time switches – an antique – it might even be valuable! I could sell it to the Science Museum for hundreds of pounds. Old Hamish McKay might have been some really famous bloke for all I know, like – well – like some other really famous inventor.

He turned it over.

But how does it connect to whatever you want switching on or off, then? The bottom of the box is fixed with screws. No plug or socket. No wires. No leads. How does it work? And why the strap?

He held it to his ear and gave it a shake.

Dad'll know, if I can get him to take an interest.

Nathan jumped up. He reset each dial to OFF and flicked the switch up. Then he moved each pointer hand, switched on and pressed the brass button. His head began to hum.

Be wary, Nathe.

His whole body began to vibrate.

"Yeow!" he cried, letting go.

It works all right, but how? Feels as if *I've* been switched on.

He blinked away the dancing colours and sparks that were having a party behind his eyeballs.

Must be a loose connection somewhere.

Nathan the Wary decided to leave it alone for the time being. He refitted the lid and shoved it in his backpack.

Still only 4.42. He leaned against the wall, hugging

15

himself to keep warm. A large drop of rain dribbled down his collar.

What to do then? Gav's at school badminton club – he always is these days. Hardly ever see Sime – hangs around with a different crowd now. What about Nan's?

He set off, thinking about the evening ahead, alone with Dad. It loomed like a dark, gathering cloud.

"Yeah, he's doing great," Nathan had lied to Mum about Dad, many times. This had been . . .

Plan B: SUPERDAD/SUPERCOOK/LIFE AND SOUL OF THE PARTY

ACTION: Lie.

LIE 1: It's all wonderful at Bryjan.

LIE 2: Dad and me have a great time. It's a laugh a minute.

LIE 3: You don't know what you're missing, Mum.

AIM: Make Mum want to come back.

MUM'S RESPONSE: (not even looking up from her newspaper) "Sounds like he's had a personality transplant, Nathan. Well, I'm pleased to hear it, for your sake. He's terrible to live with when he's in one of his silent sulks." (Then, looking up and smiling) "See? It's better for both of us this way, Nathan."

RESULT: Failure.

Plan A: WHO ARE YOU? I DON'T RECOGNISE YOU. OH YES – DIDN'T YOU USED TO BE MY MOTHER? had been the first plan to go down the drain though. It hadn't really been a plan. It had just happened. He couldn't help himself. Not after she just left like that. Not when he worked out she must have been planning it for ages. Why hadn't she told him? She could have at least told him.

ACTION: Ignore her.

Even when she waited for him outside school and tried to talk to him. He'd walked past her. Even when she kept ringing up. He'd hung up. Even when she wrote to him:

> *Dear Nathan, I didn't mean for it to happen like this. Please try and understand . . .*

He'd torn it up.

RESULT: Failure.

He couldn't keep it up. He found himself outside her flat one evening and rang the doorbell. She'd cried. He'd cried. A right blubby pair. He'd stayed the night. When he rang Dad to explain, there'd been a long silence. "I see, Nathan," he'd said at last. And put the phone down. Nathan the Traitor. Now he shared his time between them. *Doyng! Doyng!*

Also a complete waste of brain power:

Plan C: WATCH OUT, MUM – DAD'S A LADY-KILLER. GET BACK THERE QUICK, BEFORE IT'S TOO LATE.

ACTION: Make Mum dead jealous.

1. Tell the truth.

"There was this woman round Dad's last night. I think her name's Debbie. Really nice. Wavy blonde hair. She's coming round again tonight. I wonder what it's like having a stepmother? She's really young looking."

2. Don't tell the complete truth. That is:

"I know her name's Debbie because it was printed on the

identity badge she was wearing, and she was rattling a collecting tin for Help the Aged, and Dad said he didn't have any change and when she said, 'Don't worry, I'll call back tomorrow night', he was really grumpy about it."

AIM: Get Mum back – fast.

MUM'S RESPONSE: "Really? Your Dad? You do surprise me. Well, the best of luck to Debbie, whoever she is."

RESULT: Failure.

And he should have guessed, even before he'd started on ...

Plan D: LOOK, MUM, DAD'S DEAD MISERABLE AND IT'S ALL YOUR FAULT. YOU'VE GOT TO DO SOMETHING! PLEASE! COME BACK! that it would never have worked.

MUM'S RESPONSE: "Look, Nathe, if I come back they'll be two of us dead miserable. Is that what you want?"

It would have to be Plan E next. The trouble was he hadn't thought of it yet.

"Hello, Nathan!" said Nan, opening her door. "You've grown!"

"You only saw me last week, Nan."

"Must be all this rain," said Nan. "Come on in then, love. Look at you – all soaked through."

She tutted around him. Took off his coat and turned on the gas fire, and hung the coat over a chair to dry.

This was more like it. Good old Nan. Comforting sounds travelled from the kitchen. The kettle boiling, plates rattling, the scrape of the cake tin on the worktop. He

18

snuggled into the cushions of Nan's sofa with a contented sigh.

"Here we are then," she said, carrying in a loaded tray. "Sorry, love, only jam sponge today. Chocolate fudge is your favourite, isn't it?"

"I'll manage. Thanks, Nan."

"How's your Mum?"

"All right."

"And how's my favourite grandson?"

"Aw-ry," shrugged her only grandson, with a mouthful of cake. "I'm staying at Dad's tonight," he added when he could speak properly.

"He's lucky to have you, Nathan. I can't get through to him at all. I've told him – get out – get busy – take your mind off things. That's what I had to do when your grandad died. It's no good sitting at home brooding and feeling sorry for yourself. Waste of breath though. The pair of them need their heads banging together if you ask me."

She poured herself another cup of tea.

"Not that I'm taking sides, Nathan. It takes two to tango. Remember, no one's perfect, Nathan. Ooh. Look at the time. Turn *Neighbours* on for me, Nathan, there's a love."

"I better go," said Nathan reluctantly after a while. "Dad'll be home soon. Bye, Nan. Thanks for the tea."

"Bye, love," said Nan, reaching up for a kiss. "Now look at that." She pointed at the television screen. "I've been looking everywhere for a lampshade like that."

*

Nan's right, thought Nathan as he headed back to Bryjan. Dad needs to pull himself together. He's not exactly Action Man at the moment, is he? More like Zombie Man. No chance at all of Mum coming back, not while he's like this. Something's got to be done about Dad first.

It came to him just as he turned the corner of Oaklands Road.

Plan E: BRINGING THE DEAD – DAD – BACK TO LIFE

ACTION: Get Dad motivated.

1. Suggest a few odd jobs that need doing round the house. Something to get the old Black and Decker whirring again.

2. A new home-improvement project.

Don't I remember Dad going on about rigging up a burglar deterrent system – something to do with lights coming on and off and recordings of dogs barking? It'll need a time switch, won't it? And haven't I just found the very thing to get him started? McKay's Automatic Time Dial Apparatus! Just what he needs to get him out of his armchair, take his mind off things.

Nathan couldn't wait to get going. As Dad's car turned into Bryjan's drive, Nathan bounded towards him.

"Hi, Dad!" he yelled.

"Don't tell me you've forgotten your key again," said Dad, slamming the car door.

"Who, me?" grinned Nathan. "Nah."

"Here, Dad, you ought to do something about that," said

Nathan, as they ate their fish and chips in front of the television. He pointed his chip to the flap of peeling wallpaper next to the radiator. It had taken him ten minutes working away with the egg slice and a wet dishcloth to get it loose, while Dad had been at the chip shop.

Dad gave an uninterested glance at the wallpaper and flicked TV channels with the remote control.

This is serious. Condition critical. Is this the man who used to check everything twice with a spirit level and a plumb line?

"In fact I think this whole room could do with a change. They've got a sale on at Fads this week – and there's a huge packet of Polycell in the shed. What about that new steam paper-stripper – you only used it once – I could help if you like – how about red . . .?"

"Where exactly is it your Mum's gone then, Nathan?" said Dad without taking his eyes from the screen.

"I dunno. Something to do with her job. A training day, I think."

"Well, just tell her from me, will you, it's time she sorted herself out? These hotchpotch arrangements won't do. It's you I'm thinking of. All this to-ing and fro-ing – it's not on, Nathan. It can't be doing your school work any good either. Has she thought of that? You'd be better off here, Nathan. If she wants to see you, then she's got to be more organised about it. I'm not having it."

Nathan concentrated very hard on cutting a large chip into small pieces.

"It's that job of hers, that's what started all this," Dad

continued. "From the moment she got that job, nothing else mattered. But, if that's what she wants" – he waved a fork in the air – "fine by me. She knows she can come back any time she likes – just say the word. And what's she doing in that poky flat when she's got all this?"

"I dunno," muttered Nathan again.

Somehow Mum seemed quite happy in her shabby little flat with its grotty furniture.

Poor old Dad. It's not fair. All that work he's put in. And she *does* go on about her job. And, yeah, what about me and my school work? I'll remember that next time I get an earful for late homework. Why can't we be like we were before? All together.

"I need another shelf in my room, Dad," said Nathan, trying to resuscitate Stage One of Plan E.

Dad pressed the remote control. A cow danced across the screen, holding hands with a jar of mustard. It flicked to Mr Spock of the Starship Enterprise. "May I respectfully remind you, Captain . . ."

Flick to view of Buckingham Palace.

Flick into a scene of people lying dead on a pavement somewhere.

"Do you think you could do that, Dad? Fix me another shelf . . ."

"What?"

"A shelf. In my room. . ."

"They ought to get rid of him. He doesn't know what he's talking about," said Dad as the face of a prominent MP loomed onto the screen. "Rubbish – you don't know how the other half lives," Dad told the prominent MP.

"I could really use another shelf, Dad."

"Yes, all *right*, Nathan."

The body-covered pavement flicked back onto the screen.

"Can we watch *Star Trek*, Dad?"

Dad didn't hear. Nathan finished his chips and went into the kitchen. He grabbed a spoon from the draining board and spoke into it, addressing his reflection in the window glass.

Now over to our reporter at Oaklands Road: "Life is much calmer at Bryjan since Mrs Janice Beazer took up position in Flat 2A, 295 London Road. But it's an uneasy peace and negotiations have broken down since Mrs Beazer refuses to discuss a reconciliation. As is often the case, it is the innocent bystander who suffers. The children and the old . . ."

He threw the spoon into the sink.

What right have I to feel miserable? At least *they* aren't lying dead on a pavement somewhere, are they?

He went off to shoot aliens on his Nintendo. You could bring them back to life when you switched on again. Unlike the News.

As an alien spacecraft ruptured his communications system, he remembered.

I haven't played my masterstroke, have I? McKay's Time Dial Apparatus.

He fetched the box from his bag, cleaned it up with the

dishcloth and strolled into the sitting room. Dad was slumped in front of a programme about knitting.

"Hey, Dad, I found something really interesting today. I think it might be a sort of time switch. It's got dials and things – look! What d'you think, Dad?"

He removed the lid and held the box out.

For a moment Dad looked interested. He gave it a quick look over, then gave a snort.

"This is ancient, Nathan. Where did you find it?"

"In a skip, down by —"

"Best place for it probably."

"It's not a time switch, then?"

"How could it be? Use your head, Nathan. Where would it connect? Where's the power source? What do they teach you in school these days?"

"No good for setting up a burglar deterrent system, then?"

"You've got to be joking."

"What is it then?"

Dad shrugged and reached for the *Radio Times*.

"I thought you'd be interested, that's all, Dad. It does *something*. When I was playing around with it, it started humming."

"Why do they put so much rubbish on telly these days?" said Dad.

"Don't you even want a little look, Dad? It does some pretty weird things – and you always say you like to know what makes things tick. Dad? Never mind," he sighed, putting the lid back on the box.

24

Out in the hall, he put down his box, reached for the machine gun slung over his shoulder, swung round, gun grasped in both hands and silently panned the room. Then he aimed it at Dad.

It's the only way, Dad. Sorry. Best to get it over with.

He swung to the right and pointed it dead centre of the television screen. And fired.

K-k-k-k-k-k-k! K-k-k-k-k-k-k! K-k-k-k-k-k-k!

Bull's-eye. It burst into flames.

He tossed the smoking gun to the ground, picked up his box and slowly climbed the stairs to his room.

"Widget! It's got a widget!" sang the television.

Nathan couldn't find his painted brick. He'd wanted to stick it on the wall above his shelf. A large part of his life was here on this shelf. The matchbox containing all his old teeth. His first swimming certificate: 10 METRES UN-ASSISTED DOGGY PADDLE. A strip of yellowing Sellotape stuck with the nine stitches removed from his knee, age seven, from the time Gav demonstrated how easy it was to ride down Gravel Hill with Nathan on the handlebars. His Womble egg cup containing scab from said knee. His three-legged stuffed stoat. His five fossils. His rock that looked like an elephant. His photobooth snap of the Fearless Four; well Fearless two and a half really. Sime was hidden behind Gav, and Nick bent down just as the bulb flashed. But you could see they were all having a good time.

"This is your life, Nathan Beazer," he announced as he

made a space for McKay's Time Dial Apparatus on his shelf. Then he picked it up again, looped the strap over his head and removed the lid. He turned each pointer on the dial, flicked down the switch and pressed the button.

His head hummed gently. A swooping hum, rising and falling, diving and swerving, loud then faint, as if searching for something. But no sparks this time, no lights, no powerful vibrations. He took his finger off the button and redialled. Again, just the singing, searching hum. And again and again, each time he tried. It was getting dark now. He moved to the door and switched on the light. The shadowy letters scratched below the dials showed more clearly under the light. He squinted closely at them. The large dial at the top was marked and numbered from nought to twenty-four. The word *Hours* was etched above it.

Day   Month   Year: Hundreds   Year: Tens and Units, he read slowly above the row of smaller dials. The *Day* dial was numbered from one to thirty-one and the *Month* dial from one to twelve. The first of the *Year* dials was numbered from ten to twenty, and the second *Year* dial from nought to ninety-nine.

Idly, he pressed the button again.

The swooping hum filled his head.

But this time it found what it was searching for. Suddenly, it settled on a vibrant note and locked into it, sending tremors throughout his body.

You've got to be bold, Nathan. But be wary.

For half a second his finger wavered uncertainly on the button as the lights started playing behind his eyeballs.

Nathan the Bold forced his finger down onto the button. Slowly, the lights faded. The hum vanished. He blinked. He could see quite clearly. Nothing had happened. He was in his room. He still had two legs and two . . .

Hang about!

His legs were bare and ended in feet wearing – purple sandals! There was nail varnish on his toes, too. And wasn't that a glimpse of flowery skirt around his knees? He was walking across the room now – towards his own bed – and he couldn't stop himself. Somehow his bed had acquired a Thomas the Tank Engine cover. What's more, there was someone in his bed. *His* bed!

"Oi, what you doing in my bed?" he said, but his voice sounded like a distant echo and the body in the bed took no notice at all. Next thing, he was bending over the bed.

"Nighty-night. Sleep tight. Don't let the bedbugs bite," he heard himself say. But it wasn't his voice.

The body in the bed, turned over, grinned, grabbed him round the neck and gave him a big wet kiss.

"G'night, Mummy," said the body.

As he drew back he saw a small boy's face smiling up at him.

Oh my . . . I recognise that face! And that red hair. Titian, to be exact. That's me, isn't it? How old was I then? I remember the Thomas the Tank Engine cover now, and the E.T. pyjamas. Walking back to the door. Can't think – too much happening. I want another look at me in bed – but I can't turn. Then in comes Dad – a younger Dad – and he goes over to the bed, and he's making the bed bounce and the me in the bed is giggling like mad and shouting, *"Stop, Dad, stop!"*, but I know he doesn't mean it. Then suddenly he does stop, because the me in the skirt and the purple sandals is saying, *"Bryan, don't do that – you'll get him overexcited."* Now I'm reaching out to the light switch, but it's not my hand – it's got rings on. Walking out on to the landing ...

"Nathan!" called Dad's voice.

I can hear him, but like he's miles away, like he's calling from the depths of a cave.

"Nathan!"

He released the button. And instantly he was back in his room. Standing exactly where he'd begun, by the light switch, the strap around his neck, the box hanging in front of him, his hands still grasping the box. The light was on. His red and blue stripy cover was back on his bed. His bed was bodiless.

"Nathan?" called Dad from the bottom of the stairs. "I'm making some tea – want some?"

"Er, yeah. Thanks, Dad."

He stared at his bed. He stared at the box.

You were wrong, Dad. This doesn't belong in a skip. I don't know what it is exactly, but whatever it is, it's amazing.

He flicked the switch up into its off position and studied the dials. Day: 2   Month: 6   Year: 1989.

I was six years old then. I think I've just seen myself, six years old – through Mum's eyes. That's who I was. Mum! Somehow I switched into Mum – six years ago – saying

28

goodnight to me. And saw Dad giving me the goodnight bounce. I'd forgotten about the goodnight bounce – when did he stop doing that? And I heard Dad calling too – the now Dad – in the present. A long way off, yeah, but I heard him. Somehow, I was in two time zones – two bodies – all at the same time.

Wrong again, Dad. This *is* a time switch. Better than any time switch you can buy at Dixons. This doesn't switch *things* on. It switches *people* on and switches them back in time. I've just travelled backwards six years. And it's more than just a time switch. It's a *person* switch. For a couple of minutes I wasn't me. I was Mum. I was Mum *and* me, looking at me. Six years ago I was kissed by me! I think.

He switched on and pressed the button again.

Here I go – walking across the room – big wet kiss – back to the door . . .

Nathan released the button.

I didn't imagine it, did I? I've just repeated it. I could repeat it over and over if I wanted – like a video – just by setting the time dials.

Wow! It opens up endless possibilities. Can't think of them all just at this moment, but I will. Just now, my head can't take any more in.

He felt wonderful. Lit up. Buzzing. He jumped on the bed and bounced.

"For heaven's sakes, Nathan, what are you doing up there?" Dad called from below. "And what about this tea? It's going cold!"

*

29

He couldn't sleep. He felt he could leap canyons, hurl boulders, climb Everest. Backwards.

Trouble is, there's a severe shortage of canyons, boulders and mountains round here.

His head replayed the switchback, then suddenly he was drifting into a dark place.

Someone's hammering – it's coming from outside – coming from a door – like it's being nailed up or something. Dark and smelly inside, surrounded by groaning, writhing bodies, someone shouting – outside I think – *"Plague house! Keep away!"* Oh no! I must have switched back to the time of the Plague. How did that happen? Did I roll over on the switch in bed or something? Quick – where is it? Find it – quick! Switch back to me! What's happening? The button's stuck! Flicking the switch, turning the dials – nothing works! Hammering the button – won't budge! Can't get back – stuck in time – I'm dying ... Help! Let me out! I don't belong here! It's all a mistake! Help me! Aaaaagh ...

He jolted awake, hot, sweating and heaving.

It was a nightmare! Just a nightmare! You haven't switched, Nathe. You're in bed. It's OK. It's OK.

His heart felt as if it too was hammering to get out.

He turned on his lamp. The switch was where he'd left it, at the end of the bed. He checked himself for lumps and spots. Flopped back onto his pillow.

You're going to have to be very wary with this switch, Nathe, very wary indeed. Could be dodgy. Deadly dodgy.

He decided to leave his bedside lamp on.

The next thing he knew, hundreds of tiny little Nathans, all wearing E.T. pyjamas, were climbing out of the box and tugging the covers off him.

"Get off! Leave me alone!" he shouted pulling it over his head.

But it was only Dad.

"Don't just lie there, Nathan. Get going! It's nearly eight o'clock. You're going to be late for school."

"It's part of my Energy Saving Drive," groaned Nathan.

3
~
A Day in the Life of Nathan
Beazer – Part One
~

It's not real, thought Nathan as he dressed. There's no such thing as a time switch that switches you back in time. It's all a dream – and I'm still in it. Any minute now a gorilla in a Kung Fu suit will leap from the wardrobe, grab me under his arm and swing from the light fitting out of the window.

This was one of Nathan's recurring dreams.

But the jarring of the school bell as he arrived at the gates, the push and shove of the corridors and the smell of the boys' cloakrooms told him. Yeah. This is reality.

"Baker, Ball, Beazer ... Beazer? Anyone seen Nathan Beazer?"

"He's here, Mrs Hawkins," someone said.

"Wake up, Nathan," said Mrs Hawkins. "Registration will take all day if everyone's like you."

"What would you say if I told you that I'd discovered a switch that could take you back in time?" Nathan asked Gav at break. "Not only that, but in the body of another person. Eh? What would you say?"

"I'd say you were stark raving bonkers," said Gav, draining the contents of a crisp bag into his mouth.

"Thought you would," said Nathan.

"What sort of question's that, anyway?" said Gav.

"Just an idea, just an idea," said Nathan, narrowing his eyes and tapping the side of his nose knowingly.

"Sounds all right," said Gav. "I could be Linford Christie winning the gold at Barcelona!" He ran on the spot, punching the air with a fist.

"Neil Armstrong walking on the moon," announced Nathan. " 'That's one small step for man – one giant leap for mankind,' " he drawled in an American accent, going into slow-motion replay.

They were halted by a chorus of howling laughter from a group of girls, pointing at them.

"Nathan – one and a half!" cried Sarah.

Great guffaws of laughter.

"I think we're in the minuses here," yelled Nickie.

General collapse into giggling and leaning on each other's shoulders for support as they pointed at Nathan and Gav; Sarah and Nickie and Tansy and Nina.

"What about Gav, then?" said someone.

"Be generous – he's got a nice bum," giggled Tansy.

"Two and a half, then!" yelled Sarah.

The four girls doubled over, screeching and clasping their ribs.

"Leave my bum out of it," said Gav. "It's private."

The girls were hysterical now. What were they on about? One thing was certain. The boys were the joke. Only *they* couldn't see the funny side.

Nathan felt himself turning pink. Strawberry, cerise, carnation, fuchsia, beetroot, red, red for danger, spewed his

33

memory banks. WARNING! WARNING! Alien fleet poised to attack. EMERGENCY! Retreat! Retreat!

"Come on," mumbled Gav. "Let's get out of here."

"Charisma!" shouted Nickie. "Know what that is? We're giving scores out of ten . . ."

Paroxysms of laughter as they walked away.

"Gavin Prentice!" shouted Mr Onslow. "Don't leave your crisp packet there!"

"But it's not mine . . ."

"I don't care whose it is. Go back, pick it up, dispose of it – in a bin."

"Yes, Mr Onslow."

"What were they on about?" muttered Gav as they crossed to the bin.

"Something called krisma," said Nathan.

"Sounds like a disease," said Gav.

"Or an aftershave," said Nathan.

"Anyway, I don't want it, do you?" said Gav.

"Nah. Whatever it is."

"Just imagine," said Mr Onslow, spreading his arms as he leaned against his desk, "what it must have been like. There you are, going about your normal business – a simple Saxon peasant farmer perhaps, eking a living from the land, or a housewife – spinning, weaving, selling a few goods at the market, or a child – helping on the land and at home. Maybe a rich merchant even, when suddenly – invasion. Invasion, and terror, and – for many – death."

34

He scanned the faces of the class to make sure he had their full attention.

"An army of hard, fierce men in chain mail, faces hidden beneath iron helmets, storm the town. They come on horses, on foot, on boats along the river. They shout commands at you in a language you don't understand. They take your houses, your lands. They strike down anyone who resists. They strike down those that don't resist — as a reminder that they are now your masters. You learn to obey very quickly. For they are ruthless. They come with swords, and knives and axes. They hack and burn their way across the country, destroying anyone who defies them. (Thank you, Steven. I think we can manage without the mad axe man demonstration.) They seek bloody revenge on rebels and uprisings. They build fortresses and castles to subdue and rule. They are — the Normans."

Mr Onslow paused, giving time for them to imagine all the dreadful things the Normans were going to do to them if they weren't careful.

"Just listen to this," he continued, picking up a book. "This was written in 1109 about King William's revenge for a Saxon rebellion against the Norman governor of York in 1069: 'Swift was the King's coming and nowhere did William show more cruelty. He cut down many in his vengeance. And then, in his anger, he commanded that all crops and herds, food of every kind, be burned, to strip the land of its goodness.'"

He threw the book back onto the desk.

"Indeed, all the villages between York and Durham were destroyed. There were no people left. William ordered that every man, woman and child be hunted down and killed. If anyone had managed to survive the slaughter, they would have starved to death."

There was total silence in the room. Steven lolled lifelessly in his chair, mouth open, tongue hanging out.

"And yet ..." Mr Onslow went on, clapping his hands together, "... these were the same men who built our magnificent cathedrals, introduced new laws, new fashions, encouraged artistry. In time, Saxon and Norman learned to live together, intermarry, speak the same language. They saw themselves as scholars, builders, architects and Christians."

He levered himself from his desk, put his hands in his pockets, stared down at his shoes thoughtfully, then suddenly looked up.

"How do we know all this? How do we know they lived here? Where's the evidence?"

Hands shot up.

"The castle, Mr Onslow."

"The Domesday Book."

"And the round arches in St Mary's ..."

"Good," said Mr Onslow after they'd regurgitated every scrap of information he'd fed them over the last half term. "Now – some real work. *You* are going to be Saxons – Saxons who have just been invaded by the bossy Normans. Be anyone you like. I want you to describe a day in the life of a Saxon. The things you've seen, the things you've heard – what you *feel*. I shall be expecting a particularly illuminating account from you, Steven, on the strength of the Thespian talents we have all been so privileged to witness."

"What?" said Steven, recovering quickly from his death by starvation.

"You can all start now by doing some research," continued Mr Onslow. "Books here, slides over there. There's a CD-ROM program set up on the computer ... Wait. Sit down, Sarah. You take it in turns – groups of four – see the list on the board. Same goes for the video programme set up in the corridor. Right – off you go. Remember. See it through their eyes."

See it through their eyes, thought Nathan. I wonder ... If only you knew, Mr Onslow. If only you knew about the switch. That's if I didn't imagine it. But if I didn't – if it's real – I could really see it through their eyes, couldn't I? If it switches back that far. Bit iffy. Could end up being hacked to death by some Norman. Better start brushing up on the French. *'Je suis* Nathan Beazer. *Un sandwich au jambon, s'il vous plaît.'* But would I need it? When I spoke last night, they didn't hear me, did they? It was Mum speaking. But what if ...?

"Come along, Nathan. Don't sit there dreaming."

Nathan fetched a book and flicked the pages.

Anyway, what suddenly triggered the switch last night? I pressed the button loads of times on the same settings – nothing happened. What switched me into Mum, six years ago? And what if it jammed, like the dream. Dodgy.

Definitely dodgy. Shut up, Nathe. You're going crazy. You must have imagined it.

No you didn't, said another part of him.

That proves it. You are crazy, said the other part.

He yawned. He'd felt tired all day. It was an effort to think or move; like swimming through treacle.

"Right, listen everyone," said Mr Onslow. "Homework: first draft of your 'Day in the Life of a Saxon' assignment. By next Monday, please."

Nathan groaned. He'd got E+ last time. With a note: "I have been generous with the grading considering that you managed to hand it in on time this week. Please may we have a little more than fifteen and a half lines next time, Nathan? Without the biscuit crumbs."

The bell signalled end of lesson.

"Everything back where you found it, please," said Mr Onslow. "Nathan, Gavin, Steven, Tim — stay behind, will you, and make sure everything's where it should be? I'm on duty."

"What's the point of all this?" said Gav, stacking the books. "I mean — what's the good of history?"

"Yeah," agreed Nathan. "What's it for? You can't use it for anything, can you?"

"It's not going to get you a job, is it?" said Tim.

"Imagine you're a Saxon," mimicked Steven. "I can think of better things to use my imagination on, thanks very much."

"Yeah, but *you'll* be history if you don't do it. Onslow's diabolical with the detention slips," said Gav.

"You might even be geography," said Tim.

"Geography?" they chorused. "What you on about? How could you be geography?"

"Like spread across five counties," explained Tim.

"Or biology if you're not careful," said Nathan.

"Biology?"

"He'll dissect you piece by piece in front of the class."

"Here, speaking of dissection, look at this," said Tim, pointing to a page illustrating medieval forms of torture.

"Ugh," said Gav. "It's disgusting. Is there any more? Look over the page. Cor! I'm glad they don't still do that."

"Only if you don't do your homework," said Tim.

"Mine'll be brilliant," said Steven. "What with all my Thespian talents."

"What does that mean?" asked Gav.

"Don't ask me. All I know is I've got them."

"Oh no," sighed Nathan as they made their way to the changing rooms. "I think I've left my football kit at Mum's."

"Death by a hundred laps round the field for you," said Gav.

"Not again, Beazer," said Mr Cosby when he told him. "Are you deliberately trying to annoy me?"

"No, Mr Cosby. It's just that ..."

"There's spare kit in the cupboard. Hurry up, Beazer. We haven't got all day."

In boots two sizes too big, odd socks, flapping shorts that reached his knees and a shirt that smelt like very old wellingtons, Nathan trudged his way wearily across the rain-soaked field.

CRASH!

"Come on, Nathe, lend a hand."

"What? What?"

Mum was backing through the front door of the flat, dragging a large cardboard box.

He rubbed his eyes, trying to work out where he was; who he was. He was lying on the sofa in the flat. He looked at his watch. He'd been asleep. For over an hour. Dreaming of the Normans landing on the moon in the Starship Domesday.

4
~

A Day in the Life of Nathan
Beazer – Part Two
~

"Do that again, Nathan," said Mum.

"Do what?"

"Walk – walk across from me to the door."

Nathan limped to the door.

"Come here. Let me look at that leg."

She bent down and squeezed his leg.

"Pull up your trouser – I need to see it."

He pulled up his trouser.

"Now, let me look at the other one."

She squeezed that leg too.

"That's a nasty limp, Nathe."

"Is it?" said Nathan.

"This might be serious – I ought to take you to the doctor."

"It might?"

"Now where's the number?"

She was flicking through her phone pad.

"It's OK, Mum, I'll manage. I'll just lie down for a bit. I wouldn't mind a cup of tea though – and a KitKat."

He stretched out on the sofa and carefully propped his leg with a cushion.

"I think it should be looked at," said Mum, picking up

the phone. She started to press the numbers out. "If I'm not mistaken, it's a nasty case of infectious limp."

He could feel her watching him. She'd stopped dialling.

"It seems to have transferred itself from the right leg" – she was having trouble keeping a straight face – "that was giving you such problems yesterday, to the left leg today. Or hadn't you noticed?"

Now she had the expression Sherlock Holmes might have had when he solved the riddle of the Speckled Band. She slowly lowered the phone and let it drop, with a satisfied ping, into its cradle. She was laughing.

I'm going outside, Nathan wanted to say, and I may be gone some time. But it was cold and drizzly outside and a long walk down two flights of stairs. He couldn't go to his room. He didn't have one. Only the sofa bed he was sitting on.

Mum crossed to the sofa, leaned over the back and put her arms round him.

"Never mind, Nathe. It was a very good limp. Very impressive. The best I've ever seen. See – I did notice. Now, what's up?"

"Oh, nothing! Nothing at all! I just got it in the neck again 'cos I hadn't got my kit. You'd limp if you had to wear boots ten sizes too big. I've got blisters the size of jellyfish. And you forgot to give me any dinner money! I had to survive all day on a fish finger that Gav was kind enough to give me! Oh yeah – and a near-death experience in Glebe Road! Not to mention Dad who's in major decline. He says it's time you sorted yourself out. It's doing me no good at all, these hotchpotch arrangements of yours. *He's worried* – about the effect all this is having on my school work – I bet you never thought of that – he says you've got to be more organised – this grotty old flat when we could all be at home – it's stupid. He told me to tell you ..." he added, his voice trailing away.

"Just stop there, Nathan," Mum warned. She was facing him now, eyes narrowed, hand on hip, wagging a finger.

"If I hear just one more word about what your Dad thinks, let me tell you ..."

Nathan could almost hear the air pressure in the room change. The winds were gathering.

"... I mean – how dare he! How dare he!" Her hands were fists beating the rhythm of her words.

"Does he know how organised I've had to be? Has he any idea?" she interrogated.

Nathan retreated further into the sofa. He hadn't seen Mum like this for months; the weekend before she left, when Dad had asked, quite innocently he thought, "So, I suppose you call this a Sunday dinner?" And the day before, when ...

"Does he know what it's like to start with nothing – to go out and get a job – to prove what you're capable of – when you've no skills, no qualifications? To find somewhere to live? I haven't asked him for anything, not a penny. I've done it all on my own – that's what he can't take! He likes to be in control – to think I can't manage. God ..." She pulled at her hair. "He makes me so *angreeee*!"

She was cyclonic now.

43

"How dare he make me out to be the neglectful mother and himself the caring father? To think of all the times I *didn't* walk out . . ." she told the ceiling.

"Too much for him — is it? — to have his own son occasionally. Oh, Nathan, I just hope you don't grow up like . . ."

"I don't think I want to hear all this," said Nathan, burying his head in *TV Quick*.

Mum's face was white. Her fists were clenched. The air was being sucked out of the room.

"You even *sound* like him, Nathan," she said very calmly. Too calmly. Between tight lips.

It wasn't a compliment. He could tell.

She turned, hurried to her bedroom and slammed the door. An unnatural stillness hung heavy in the air.

He sat there for several minutes. Then he got up, thought better of it, sat down again and waited. He got up again and trod softly to her door. He knocked.

"Mum? All I meant was . . ."

"Don't say another word, Nathan."

He slowly made his way back to the sofa and reached for his backpack, searching for the switch. Empty aerosol can, art overall, yesterday's socks and underpants, rough book, history book, red nail varnish, eyes on springs, bag of chicken bones, old letter from school, pencil case, half a ruler, one glove, magic putty, *very* old letter from school, plastic bag with remains of cheese sandwich — *lichen green* — maths book, science book, school tie with Peter Young

name-tag (who was Peter Young?), three empty crisp bags —
but no switch. He was sure he'd put it in. It must be still at
Dad's. He had to get over there — quick.

"I'm not going to let this spoil my day, Nathan," Mum
told him, coming out of her room. "Everything was going
wonderfully up till half an hour ago. I was in a really good
mood till then. I'm not going to let your father ruin my
day. I'm going to be calm. Perfectly calm."

She marched to the kitchen corner and slammed a frying
pan on to the hob.

"Well, Nathan? Aren't you going to ask how I got on?"

"Er — yeah — how did it go — er — your training day?"

Mum turned.

"Not a training day, Nathan. A buying trip. You didn't
listen. I hope deafness isn't an inherited condition, from
father to son."

"I forgot," he lied.

"Come here," she said. "I want to show you something."

She bent down and hauled out the large cardboard box.

It was full of packages wrapped in paper.

"This is so exciting, Nathe," she said rubbing her hands
together.

"Now ..." She lifted one of the packages and unwrapped
it carefully on to the worktop.

"Just look at that — isn't it beautiful? What d'you think,
Nathe?"

It was a bird. Or was it a pot? It was both. A pot shaped
like a plump, curving bird. Its head and tail were the

handles. Its lustrous reds and browns were etched in patterns of wings and feathers.

"And look at this."

This time it was a pot shaped like a head wearing an elaborate headpiece. Its red clay glowed. The headpiece was patterned with dark lines and swirls.

"This is the lid – see?" said Mum, lifting the headpiece off by a plume.

"They're brilliant. Where d'you get them?"

"A tiny pottery in Dorset, called Pot Peru. All their designs are based on old Peruvian pottery – you know, South America. Look – there's more."

She unwrapped pots and bowls and bottles in the shapes of fish and parrots and plump, childlike figures and strange exotic creatures.

"I persuaded Mr Leadbetter – you know, manager of the china department – to let me go and bring some samples back. Those hand-painted bowls I got him to order from that little pottery in Woodthorp have been incredibly popular. We can't get enough of them. I'm sure there's a market for this sort of thing – original, hand-made, crafted pots. I can't wait to show him. Better than all those ghastly ornaments of ladies in crinolines, and puppies and china posies in china baskets. I'm so excited, Nathe ..." She was stroking the pot as if it were a real bird.

Nathan was thinking of china ladies in crinolines and china baskets with posies of china flowers. The ones that Dad had bought her every Christmas and birthday since he could remember. They sat on the glass shelves in the alcoves at Bryjan, gathering dust now. The alcoves that Dad had fitted for her, with spotlights that he'd fitted for her. She'd never even liked them. How come Dad never knew?

"Right. What's it going to be, Nathe?" said Mum as she folded them back into their wraps. "Eggs and beans OK?"

"I'm in a hurry," said Nathan. "I left something at Dad's and I need it for my homework."

"No need to rush. I'll give you a lift if you like."

"What – piggyback?"

"Very funny. No. I'm having a driving lesson."

"But you said it would cost too much."

"A friend's teaching me," said Mum, setting down a plate of eggs and beans before him.

"Like who?" asked Nathan.

"Just an old schoolfriend," said Mum.

"Aren't you having anything to eat, Mum?" asked Nathan.

"No, I'll eat later. It's part of the deal – one driving lesson in exchange for supper."

"Mum, what's krisma?" mumbled Nathan, with a mouthful of beans.

"Krisma? You don't mean charisma, do you? What funny questions you come up with, Nathe. Well, it's – mmmm, let's think – it's like a sort of power, the sort that attracts other people to you, makes them like you, want to be with you – that sort of thing. Why d'you want to know, Nathe?"

"No particular reason," said Nathan gloomily, recalling his one and a half out of ten.

"Mum, does Dad have charisma?"

47

Mum's eyebrows nearly took off. She opened and shut her mouth several times.

"It's not a word that immediately springs to mind, Nathe," she said eventually as she wiped down the worktop.

"But he must have had it once," said Nathan. "You must have really liked him once, wanted to be with him, or you wouldn't have married him, would you?"

"Have you been using paint on this worktop again?" said Mum, scrubbing at a stain.

"Go on, Mum, tell me," he begged. "Was it his bulging biceps, Mum? Or his hairy chest? I know – it was his Black and Decker."

"What's all this about, Nathe?" she grinned.

Nathan shrugged. "Just asking."

A car hooted from the street below. Mum went to the window and waved.

"He's here. Are you ready, Nathan? I'll just get my bag . . ."

Nathan peered down into the street. A man in jeans and a leather jacket was leaning against a car. He looked up and waved. It was Tansy's old dad. What was he doing here . . .?

A horrible feeling spread inside him, as if a cold hand was squeezing his intestines.

"Mum, *that's* not your driving instructor, is it? Tell me it isn't . . ."

"What's wrong?" she said, grinning through the window. She gave another friendly wave.

"But that's Tansy's old dad! I'll never live it down. He's

not coming here, is he? You're not going to cook for him in our flat – it's gross! You can't, Mu—"

"For heaven's sake, Nathan, I'm not eloping – I'm having a driving lesson, I told you – he's an old schoolfriend, that's all. He's being very generous . . . Now come on."

"I'm not coming."

"Don't be so stupid! Move!"

Nathan slouched in the back seat.

"Cheer up, mate, it may never happen," said Tansy's dad.

The car smelt of aftershave. Nathan grasped his throat, made choking noises, flapped his hands, opened both windows, stuck his head out and took great gasps of air. Mum sat in the passenger seat. Through the rear mirror she glared at him.

"*Automag* said these cars are crap," said Nathan, who had never read *Automag*. Mum's eyes glowed like lasers. He didn't care.

The car stopped outside Bryjan.

"Here you are then," said Tansy's dad. "Jan, want to take over driving now?"

Mum slid into the driver's seat. Tansy's dad was already opening the door for him. He levered himself out.

"Here, Nathe," said Tansy's dad quietly, giving him a nudge, "up with liver, eh?"

He chuckled to himself and got in beside Mum. He said something to her and she laughed. Tansy's old dad worked in the car repair shop that backed onto Bakery Lane. He remembered now.

49

"Nought out of ten!" he shouted at the car as it crept away.

It was still only 5.37. Dad wasn't home yet. He found the switch under his bedcover. He headed back to Mum's flat. It was time to experiment. Dodgy or not. He was feeling reckless. Serve Mum right if he was hacked to death by a Norman:

"And over to our newsdesk for a newsflash:

"Mystery surrounds the slaughter of a twelve-year-old home-alone boy discovered by his mother on return to her flat this evening. The boy had apparently fought his attackers with extreme cunning, skill and bravery but detectives are puzzled by the murder weapon found on the scene. According to experts it appears to be a genuine Norman battle sword dating back to the eleventh century. The boy, home-alone Nathan Beazer, had skilfully managed to dodge the hail of arrows, the charge of horses, the spears and the axes, but was struck from behind when his defences were down. 'It's a well-known fact that the Normans were quite ruthless,' said Mr Onslow, Nathan's history teacher. His tearful mother admitted, 'It was all my fault ...'"

Yeah. Serve her right.

5

~

A Day in the Life of Nathan Beazer – Part Three or Three Lives in the Day of Nathan Beazer

~

Nathan stood in the middle of the room. He looped the strap over his neck and tossed the lid onto the sofa. He gazed at the dials. He wasn't feeling so reckless now. What if something *did* go wrong? Who would hear his screams for help? The students in the flat across the landing? Not over all that heavy-metal music that was thumping through the wall.

A boy has to boldly go . . .

But let's go for something not too risky. No axes, no swords, definitely no tortures. Last Sunday, 0800 hours. Should be reasonably axe-free territory. He set the dials, flicked the switch – and pressed the button.

The hum swooped and dived. But it wasn't connecting. The phone started to ring. Nathan released the button and crossed to the phone.

"Can I speak to Kevin, please? This is Lynne."

"He's not here any more."

"What, Kevin? Where's he gone then? He didn't say—"

"I dunno. We've got the flat now."

"I really need to talk to him. Have you got his number?"

"Sorry."

He put the phone down. Girls were always ringing up for Kevin. Whoever he was, *he* wasn't short of charisma.

He stabbed again at the brass button.

mmmmmmmMMMMMMMMMMMMMMMMMMMMMM.
It locked into a single note. Vibrations. Dancing lights. Colours. Fading now ...

The phone was ringing again. But the curtains were closed, leaking morning sunlight onto the carpet. Without any conscious effort he was reaching for the phone with a hand that wasn't his own.

"Hello," he yawned, pushing back long hair from his face.

"Janice?"

Feeling more awake now. Feeling cross. Not going to speak.

"I know you're there, Janice. Just listen ..."

So angry can't help self. Shout into phone.

"Bryan? Have you woken me up – just for this? I'm putting the phone down ..."

"Don't. Wait! Listen – I'm willing to have you back. We can sort it out ..."

Richter scale 8 now. Spitting out the words.

"Oh – you're willing are you? How generous of you! No thanks! I am NOT – repeat NOT – N – O – T – coming back. When – are – you – go – ing – to – get – that – in – to – your – head? When you accept that, *then* I'll talk to you."

Slam phone down. Seismic. Kick armchair. Ouch. Hurt toe.

"Now look what you've made me do!"

Hop to kettle. Turn on tap. Slam lid on. Slam mug onto worktop.

"What's up? What's going on, Mum?" yawns voice.

Turn and look at sofa bed. Tuft of hair, Titian, sticking out from horrible flowery duvet. White foot also hanging out.

"Your father, Nathan. Who else would ring at this time on a Sunday morning!"

Slam coffee jar down. Throw spoon down. Spoon bounces onto floor.

Head pokes out from duvet. Eyes like slits. Pasty face. Vertical hair. Rubs slitty eyes. Squints at sunlight. Slides back under duvet.

Nathan lifted his finger from the button of the switch. Instantly he was back standing by the phone. Nathan Beazer. Twenty past seven. Thursday evening. He'd just switched into Mum again, 8 a.m. last Sunday. He'd seen himself on the sofa bed. So why had it worked standing here – and not over there?

He walked back to the sofa and tried again. No connection. Just the swooping hum. He walked back to the phone and pressed the switch's button. Hum. Connection. Switch completed.

Ring, ring. Ring, ring.

"Hello," he yawned, pushing long hair back from his face.

"Janice?"

He released the button. Back to Nathan Beazer. Thursday. 7.22.

It's simple! It's brilliant! Old Hamish McKay was a genius! The rule is: you have to be standing in the right place, the *exact* place the person was standing at the set time. That's why the hum swooped! It was searching, trying to tune in, to – to energy – or thoughts – brainwaves – whatever. When it found it, it connected. But you have to help it. You have to stand in the right place. *You* are the receiver! When your finger's pressed on the button, you become the receiver. That's why it worked before. I'd been standing by the door – where Mum happened to be coming in. That's why I suddenly switched. But what about me – the now me – where am I when I'm switched?

Nathan positioned himself by the phone again and pressed the button.

Ring, ring. Ring, ring.

"Hello . . ."

Slam phone down. Stub toe. Kettle.

The Sunday me: "What's going on, Mum?"

Turn to look at the Sunday me.

Yeah, I can see the Sunday me poking out from the duvet and rubbing my eyes, and the phone – where I'm standing now – but *I'm* not there, not the *Thursday* Nathan. I don't exist yet.

"Your father, Nathan . . ."

Right, let's see if I can make Mum *do* something. Make her move her hand. Concentrate . . .

Harder ...

It's no good. I can't. I can see what she's seeing, hear what she's hearing, know what she's feeling, but there's no control. And listen – heavy-metal music – faint, distant, but definitely there. I'm in two time zones – past and present.

He released the button.

What next? What about switching into me, then. Last Sunday, in bed, with Mum bashing about in the kitchen.

He stretched out on the sofa. But the instant his finger pressed the button a piercing whistle screamed in his head. He had two more tries.

Aaagh! Brain-sizzling. No. Doesn't work. I can't be myself, not in the past anyway. Well, you can't phone yourself up, can you? But it's still amazing. Futuristic. Yeah, what about the future? What about next Saturday? Six o'clock, when we always have spaghetti and watch telly.

He swapped to Mum's armchair, reset the dials. Pressed the button.

Nothing. Zero. Nil. Zilch. Not even a hum.

Try Mum's bed, 6 a.m. next Sunday morning. Nothing. The kitchen corner, the phone, the bathroom. Nothing. Either it doesn't work for the future or the world's going to end before Saturday. Have to wait till Saturday to find out. Unless I'm just a puff of smoke polluting the ozone layer by then.

He suddenly noticed how dark it had become. He switched on the light. It was gone eight. He'd have one more go before Mum came home.

Where to now, then? How about switching into the charismatic Kevin? Bit risky. All those girls. It'd be kissing and stuff. No thanks. How about some time further back, now that I've got it sussed? This place must be pretty old. How about – Day: 6. Month: 2. Year: 1 – 8 – 9 – 5. Time: 21.30.

It took eleven attempts before he switched: standing just inside the front door to the flat. Doors, he was discovering, were hotspots for switching. The places where people came and went regularly. He now quickly recognised the cold spots and the early signs of a successful switch. He'd learned to be methodical, working on a grid system so he didn't waste time on the same spot more than once.

Here we go! Five, four, three, two, one ... Hum. Lights. Vibes. Hum cuts. Lights fade. We have a switch ...

Closing the door behind me. Carrying something – a tray. Oldish hands, white cuffs, black sleeves. The room's very dark, doesn't seem like the same room, bigger. Posh. Really posh. Putting tray onto round table. Look up. Big brass bed far end of room. Woman in long dark dress sitting by it, reading or something. Lights flickering on walls. Big fireplace – I don't remember a fireplace – fire burning. Boy! It's dead stuffy, smells – something sickly, flowery. And something like disinfectant.

"Oi'll leave yer supper 'ere, ma'am, shall I?" I say.

Woman looks up.

"Thank you, Bessie. It's time for mother's medicine, I think. Help me, would you?"

Walk over to bed. Tiny old lady in bed. Hardly makes a

ripple in the covers. Thin white hair on pink scalp. Lean over and hoist her up. She's like a rag doll. Stuff pillow behind her. Can see her bones.

"Come now, Mother, time for your medicine. Open her mouth, Bessie."

Ease mouth open – pink gums – toothless. She looks sightlessly at me.

"That's better. Straighten the bed, Bessie, and then check the curtains. I can feel a draught."

Straightening and smoothing the bed with hands, big, rough hands. Cross to window, pull curtain back. Reflection – white cap and apron, dark dress. Round fat face, round all over. Whiteness outside. It's snow! Covering the street and roofs – everywhere. Old-fashioned street lamps. Where've the traffic lights gone? Where's the Chinese takeaway? Tug curtain across.

"And see to the fire, Bessie."

Bending over fire, prodding with big brass poker – painful – back aches, feet ache. Straighten up and try again.

"Oi'll send Jack to fetch more coal, ma'am. Will you be needing me again tonight?"

"Possibly. I'll ring down to the kitchen if there's any change."

"Yes, m'm."

Leave room. Walking on a thick carpet. Down the stairs. Hear the church clock strike ten. Polished wood and brass everywhere, rich, patterned walls, paintings on the walls – loads of them – down to the hall. Another fireplace, I think. It's not easy to see – a door – it's fading – what?

57

He'd switched back to himself, by the door of the flat. The scene of the hall had faded. Even though he still had his finger on the button. He stabbed at it – and he was Bessie again, walking in, tray in hand.

Releasing the button, he ran out of the flat, down the stairs; just bare scuffed wood now, past the other flats with their battered doors, down to the hall and past the stairs where Bessie had disappeared. He moved the dial ten minutes ahead. Swooping hum. Try twelve minutes forward, fifteen then. Here we go . . .

I'm Bessie again, from where I lost her. Much stronger picture now. Through small door at back of stairs, dimly lit, thin narrow stairs, narrow passage.

"Jack! Jack!" I call.

Into big kitchen. Dim light from lamp on table. Boy looks up from cleaning boots.

"Needing some more coal upstairs, Jack, but put kettle on first, there's a good lad. Ooh, if I don't sit down and rest my poor feet . . . Help me with my boots, Jack. Aaah, tha's better."

Putting feet up on stool – I've got big, lumpy feet. No wonder they hurt.

"I 'ope she don't 'ave me up 'alf the night agen. 'Orl right for 'er – she can take ladylike naps when she feels like it. Let's 'ave a bit o' tea first, Jack. Well – I'll tell you something – *She's* not long for this world. A bag of bones, the old lady is. There'll be a funeral within the week, mark my words . . ."

Distant clattering noises. Someone shouting. A long way off, someone shouting . . .

"Are you all right?"

Nathan lifted his finger from the button of the switch. He was standing alongside the stairs, staring at a blank wall. The wall where he'd passed through the door.

"Are you all right?"

He looked up, trying to focus. It was one of the students, leaning over the banister. The friendly one who always said hello.

"You looked miles away."

"Yeah . . . I was – er – trying to work out where this wall might have led to once. You can see the outline of a door."

"Oh, that would have been to the basement, I expect. It's a self-contained flat now. What's that you got there, then?" she said, nodding to the switch.

"Oh this – it's a – a metal detector, a very old one. I was just seeing if it worked – but it's useless. Look – see . . ."

He looked around for something metal.

"Look, if I point it at – that hinge on that door, there's nothing, see – totally useless."

"Oh, right – so it is. See you then," she said at last, clattering up the stairs.

"Yeah. Seeya."

"Wow! Triple wow!" he said out loud when she'd gone.

He leant against the wall and slid down, hands over his head trying to stop it floating away. The floor tiles were coming towards him. He closed his eyes. Slowly, his head floated back and settled. He opened his eyes. The floor was back where it belonged. He looked around at the shabby hallway, with its cracked ceiling, its missing banister rails, its grubby, patched walls. No pictures, no velvet curtain over the door – no door. No thick carpet and rugs.

He leapt up and bounded back up the stairs, threw himself onto the sofa and tried to organise his thoughts. They were coming at him from all directions, pushing one another out of the way to get attention: replays of what he'd just seen and questions. Dozens of questions. If only he could switch them off for a moment, make them line up and take their turn. His body hummed with energy, like a car revved up for a race, but no racetrack.

What d'you expect, Nathe? Being two people at the same time, you got to expect *some* side effects. Not to mention travelling back a hundred years, passing through walls ... Yeah – what happened there? I had to re-switch, didn't I? The switch's range must be quite short. It all just faded out when I got to the basement door. But no big deal. Just move position and reconnect. And wow! This house was really something then, wasn't it? They must have been really rich. They'd die if they could see it now. The fireplace has gone for a start – the kitchen corner's there now. This wall wasn't there – or the poky bathroom, or the bedroom. It was one big room. And the bed was right where – right where I'm lying now.

He shot up from the sofa like a pebble from a catapult.

Oh boy! This is where the old lady probably died. On

this very spot. I don't want to know this. There's no way I'm sleeping on that sofa there. Mum?

Hey, Mum, where are you?

The church clock struck ten. Twice in one night.

Mum should be well home by now.

He stuffed the switch back into his school bag, fetched his duvet and pillow from Mum's room and arranged a bed below the window, well away from the sofa. He tugged off his trousers, shirt and shoes and wrapped himself in his duvet. He closed his eyes.

Switch off, Nathe. Switch off. Think blue skies, think floating clouds, think ...

The old woman's face came floating up through the clouds. She smiled a ghastly, toothless, pink-gummed smile at him ...

He kneaded his eyes to rub her away. He opened them again. Even with the lights on, the room was full of shadows he'd never noticed before.

Yeah, she probably died on that very spot ...

He closed his eyes. She floated up again.

Mum! Where are you, Mum?

Take your mind off things, Nathe. What's on telly?

He leapt up and switched on.

Click

"...*where aid workers are struggling to cope with disease ...*"

Click.

"*But, Minister, Dr Clark here says that the National Health Service is failing those who are dying while they wait ...*"

Click.

"And Marion looks lovely as Donald leads her into the cha-cha, in a dress, she tells me, that her mother handstitched with over two thousand sequins . . ."

Click.

"And now the second in our new season of horror, The Return of the Dead."

Click.

Thanks a lot. I feel much better now.

He lay there, staring up at the ceiling. The cracks in the plaster gathered into a face – an old face . . .

He turned over and plunged his face into his pillow.

Where was the comforting sound of the heavy metal when he needed it? Why wasn't it thumping through the walls?

Music – good idea! – what about some music, then?

Clasping his duvet around him, he staggered to the sideboard and grabbed the cassette radio.

Tapes. Where does Mum keep her tapes? In the sideboard cupboard. *Sounds of the Seventies, Dance Yourself Fit . . . The Wall. The Wall?* Walls are becoming a major feature in my life. Could be interesting. Give it a go.

He curled up again beneath the window. The church clock struck the half hour. Half past ten.

Where *is* Mum? She should have been home ages ago. Perhaps something's happened: *Reports are coming in of a road traffic accident . . .*

Shut up, Nathe.

He plugged in the radio and pressed Play and closed his eyes.

A rippling guitar.

A throbbing beat.

A voice –

Nathan reached out and turned up the volume.

A roaring sound – like a plane.

Drums. Keyboard. The angry voice again.

The whirr of a helicopter.

The beat stabbed. The guitar vibrated, filled his head, slowly pushed out the army of questions and images fighting for space.

He rolled his head in time to the pulsing beat. Punched the air with his fists.

A chorus of voices now – angry voices, kids' voices – yelling, *"All in all – you're just another brick in the wall!"*

"All in all," he yelled, swaying arms in the air, "you're just another brick in the wall!"

Just the guitar now, soaring and vibrating.

He was on his feet, eyes closed, shoulders hunched as he held an invisible guitar, knees bent, swaying. Swaying from side to side, energised by its power, fingers of one hand sliding up and down the strings while the other strummed and plucked.

"Nathan? Nathan!"

He opened his eyes. Mum was standing in the doorway with Tansy's old dad. They were staring at him.

"What on earth do you think you're doing?" she shouted over the music. "Half-naked in front of the window – with all the lights on! Do you know you can hear that music from the hall?"

He blinked, stared down at his underpants, his bare white legs, his socked feet. Then at Mum and Tansy's dad.

"What time do you call this!" he yelled. "Do you know how worried I've been! I thought something had happened to you! You could have crashed into a bus or something! What d'you mean by coming home so late?"

The anger pulsed through him to the rhythm of the beat.

"I can't hear myself think!" cried Mum, marching over and pulling out the plug from its socket.

"And look at this room!" she accused. "What's all your bedding doing on the floor? Is that your school shirt? Why are your trousers down there? It's a tip, Nathan! I don't expect to come back to this, and" – she sniffed the air in his direction – "have you washed?" she demanded.

"Shut up! Shut up! Shut up!" yelled Nathan. "What about you? You stink! Of cigarettes and . . .!"

"That's enough, Nathan!" Mum yelled back.

"I think I'd better go," said Tansy's dad.

"No, Mike. I think Nathan ought to apologise . . ."

"Oh, it's Mike now, is it!" yelled Nathan.

"I'll see you later," said Mike. "It's best I go."

"Yeah – go," said Nathan.

"Nathan! How dare you?"

Then, when he'd gone, turning slowly and staring at him.

"How could you, Nathan? How could you?"

"How could *you*?" he cried.

He grabbed his pillow and quilt and resettled himself under the window with his back to her.

Mum stomped across the room and tugged out the sofa bed.

"I'm not sleeping there. It's haunted," he muttered.

"What's got into you, Nathan? I'm not in the mood for this," she hissed.

"Neither am I."

"Suit yourself," said Mum, marching off. "I'm going to bed. I'll speak to you in the morning. It's been a long day."

The door slammed behind her.

All in all — you're just another brick in the wall, sang Nathan's head.

6
~
Time Switch or Time Bomb?
~

"The way you behaved last night was appalling, Nathan," said Mum as she wrenched open the Cocopops.

"I can do my own breakfast, thanks," said Nathan, snatching the packet from her. He took his bowl, flopped in front of the TV and switched on.

"I'm talking to you, Nathan."

"Carry on then."

She marched across to the TV and switched it off.

"You behave like that again, Nathan, and I'm warning you . . ."

"You'll do what? Leave?"

She looked at the wall, sucked in air and, with cheeks like balloons, blew slowly out. She sounded like a tyre deflating.

"Look, Nathe," she said, busying herself with tidying up, "perhaps I should have tried to get home earlier – but I did phone – several times – to let you know. There was no answer. I guessed you must be at your dad's still, that . . ."

"Well, you guessed wrong then, didn't you?" he interrupted, carefully placing his empty bowl on the sofa arm, where he knew it would annoy her.

He heaved himself up, crossed to the radio cassette and switched on the *Wall* tape and turned up the volume.

"Turn it down, Nathan!" she shouted.

"Sorry! Can't hear you!" yelled Nathan.

With great effort, he gathered up his bedding and dumped it on the floor in Mum's room. It was all he could do to drag himself up this morning. He felt as if all his energy had drained out.

Mum was holding the tape box when he came back, staring down at it.

"I was only seventeen when I bought this," she said. She had to shout a bit.

She's trying to get round me now. Well, tough. It won't work.

He went off to brush his teeth. When he came back she was leaning out of the window doing complicated hand signals to someone on the street below.

"Well, well," said Nathan, screwing up his face and holding his nose, "if it isn't Smelly Mike himself."

"And that's another thing, Nathan," said Mum, turning. "How could you be so rude?"

"Better hurry up, Mum. He's waiting for you."

"He's only giving me a lift with the pots, Nathan, that's all," she said, tugging on her jacket. "Look, you're reading more into this than—"

"Mum, if you cut him into slices, you'd be able to read the word POSER all the way through!"

"Ha, ha," said Mum slowly as she dragged the box to the door.

"It's not funny, Mum. Dad's worth ten of him."

The tape clicked off. The doorbell rang.

67

"All right then, mate?" said Tansy's dad as he stepped in and picked up the box.

"No, actually," said Nathan. "But thanks ever so for asking. It was very kind of you."

He stared pointedly at Mum as he said it.

"Don't be childish, Nathan," said Mum as Tansy's dad disappeared with the box. She followed him, stopped at the doorway and turned.

"I'll see you later, then. How about a takeaway, eh? A Friday night special?"

She was definitely trying to get round him.

"Why ask me?" shrugged Nathan.

When she'd gone, he tipped his school bag onto the floor. He left behind the chicken bones, the aerosol can, the green sandwich and a few other non-essential items and packed some spare clothes, the switch and a few other things he'd need for the weekend at Dad's. He decided not to leave a note. He pocketed the *Wall* tape and slammed the door behind him.

"You!"

Nathan glanced over his shoulder. It was Mrs Pickford. Nit-picking Pickford.

"Yes, you! Come here."

"What's your name?"

"Nathan Beazer, Mrs Pickford."

"Class?"

"8H2, Mrs Pickford."

"Can you see that notice there, Nathan Beazer?"

"Yes, Mrs Pickford."

"Read it to me, Nathan."

"Walk," droned Nathan. "Remember – running in school causes accidents."

"What must you do, Nathan?"

"Walk, Mrs Pickford."

"What must you not do, Nathan?"

"Run, Mrs Pickford."

"Why, Nathan?" asked Mrs Pickford.

"Because running can cause accidents, Mrs Pickford."

"Exactly. Rules are there for good reasons, Nathan. Now off you go. You're late."

I am now, Mrs Pickford, thanks to you, said his head as he plodded up the empty corridor.

That's the second time this week. Bound to be a detention.

Hey! Teacher! Leave us kids alone! sang the tape in his head.

He was Nathan Beazer. 8H2. A name. A number. A brick in the wall.

"Forty-four point seven two," said someone.

"Who agrees?" said Mr Yates.

Confident hands shot up.

"Nathan?" said Mr Yates. "You appear to be the only one who doesn't agree with the answer, if we can take the absence of a raised arm as an indicator. Tell me, what answer do you have?"

"Sir?" blinked Nathan. He tried to focus on Mr Yates's

face. To bring himself back to Double Maths from the Land of the Switch and Future Explorations.

"What's your answer, Nathan?" repeated Mr Yates. "To the calculator exercise we've been working on."

Nathan stared down hopefully at his blank calculator. It stared unhelpfully back at him.

"Stand up, Nathan," sighed Mr Yates.

Nathan's chair scraped noisily in the silent room. Some faces grinned up at him with interest. Some stared down at their calculators.

"Now, let's go through it again, shall we, Nathan? Just you and me together. Class, bear with us, will you?"

Mr Yates rapidly dictated numbers and instructions. But Nathan's head seemed to have turned to cotton wool. Perhaps it's a side effect of the switch.

Doctors from around the world are puzzling over the strange phenomenon of a boy whose brain has turned into a fluffy, white substance . . . Concentrate, Nathe. Concentrate.

". . . then, finally, find the square root," said Mr Yates.

Nathan stabbed the calculator buttons.

"Now, Nathan, tell us what answer you have."

The room held its breath and waited.

"I think I've forgotten to turn it on, Mr Yates," said Nathan.

Splutters. Groans. Giggles. Gav trying to keep a straight face.

Mr Yates closed his eyes. He appeared to be in pain. He stroked his bald patch very slowly.

"Something tells me, Nathan, that you have not been

70

paying full attention," said Mr Yates, placing his calculator carefully on his desk and spending some time lining it up precisely with the edge. He leaned forward heavily and fixed Nathan with an accusing eye.

"You have wasted a great deal of our time. Do you have anything to say, Nathan Beazer?"

"Yes, Mr Yates," said Nathan.

"Well? I'm waiting," said Mr Yates.

Nathan picked up his calculator, pressed the On button, held it up and spoke.

"Beam me up, Scottie."

The room exploded with laughter.

"I see. We have a Trekkie amongst us," said Mr Yates with a grim smile when he had regained control. "Well, Nathan, or should I call you Lieutenant Beazer, there will be no mutiny aboard this starship. At break you can report to Starfleet Command for detention orders. Meanwhile, beam yourself over to the bridge desk for further instructions and extra duties. Those of you who have been paying attention, the exercises on page thirteen."

"Hey — Gav! Hang about!" called Nathan across the cloakroom at the end of school.

"Can't!" yelled Gav back. "Got badminton practice."

"Again?"

"Yeah. I'm trying for the junior county team. Mr Cosby reckons I've a good chance."

"Yeah?"

"Yeah."

"Right."

"Seeya, then."

"Yeah. Seeya."

Nathan stuffed his two detention slips into his pocket and checked again that he'd remembered the key to Dad's. But his mind was still overloaded with the switch. He could switch the switch off but he couldn't switch his thoughts off. He'd been weighing up whether he should tell Gav about it. Part of him needed to share it with someone, but part of him told him he ought to keep it to himself. There were still so many uncertainties: like, how far could it switch back? And what made it work? And would it work every time? If I told Gav and then it didn't work, I'd look a total nerd.

But just think of the possibilities! All the great mysteries of the past – solved with a flick of the switch. You could replay ancient battles. See the crowning of kings. The switch is a door to the past, not just the distant past, but the past of last year or last week, or yesterday even. You could relive history, over and over and ...

Yeah, it makes archaeological digs and dusty museums of broken pots and rusty spears even more boring – that's dead stuff. With the switch you're there – seeing it, hearing it, smelling it. Is that what Hamish McKay was trying to do? Who was he anyway?

Nathan had sneaked off to the school library at lunch time and asked Mrs Lonsdale about Hamish McKay the famous inventor. She'd looked him up in various books but he wasn't mentioned in any of them.

And what happened to Time Dial prototypes one, two and three?

He'd looked up the word 'prototype' while he was in the library and discovered it meant the first or early models.

And was there a prototype five? And how come prototype four had ended up in a skip? And how come the world didn't know about any of it? This thing was bigger than space travel. Had Hamish McKay kept it secret on purpose? Why?

And it's not just history you could use it for, is it? What about people who've gone missing. If you knew where they'd disappeared, and what time, you could just switch back and trace them, couldn't you? And what about crimes? You could prove the criminal had been there and done it – the jury could just switch back and watch. *Mr Yates, the switch finds you guilty of robbing the Bank of England on . . .*

Then there's spying! Secret weapons. Military secrets. Terrorist plots. They wouldn't be secret any more, would they? You could switch into anyone, any time, just by standing in the right place and setting the dials. All secrets revealed – where you've been, what you've done, what you said . . .

Nathan stopped and let out a long low whistle.

Boy, oh boy! This is too much. I'm carrying, I'm carrying – a time bomb! What if it got into the wrong hands? There could be world war over this. It might be able to stop wars but it could start them too. All secrets revealed! If I wanted I could switch into – into – the Prime Minister! Me, Nathan Beazer.

He realised he'd come to a halt in Bakery Lane. Underneath UP WITH LIVER, someone had scrawled AND DOWN WITH SAUSAGES.

He turned the corner into Glebe Road.

The yellow skip had been replaced by an orange one. It was empty. The top two floors of Glebe House were windowless, showing bare walls and empty doorways.

By the time he reached Bryjan, he'd decided. He wouldn't tell anyone. Not yet. Not even Gav. He'd risked his life for this switch. The least it could do was help him with his history homework. The world could wait a bit longer for McKay's Time Dial Apparatus.

7
~
Nathan the Norman
~

The front garden of Bryjan, Nathan couldn't help noticing, was sprouting a fine crop of dandelions and a particularly spectacular thistle. He let himself in and sniffed. The smell reminded him of Nick's old dog, who hated baths. In the kitchen, washing was draped over the radiator and chairs. Pink shirts, pink pyjamas, pink sheets, pink Y-fronts and Dad's red jumper.

What's going on? Since when has Dad been into pink? Is he trying to get Mum back with a bit of snazzy dressing? It won't work, Dad. I know for a fact, she hates pink.

On the table was a pile of photo albums. One lay open.

Yeah – there's the one I took of Mum and Dad by the swimming pool at the holiday camp. That's me. What a twat! Why was I wearing a false nose, swimming flippers and holding a bucket on my head? I remember – it was the obstacle race. And there we all are, on the stage in the family quiz competition. And that's my tenth birthday with Sime and Gav and the rest – that was a great laugh.

He dumped his bag by the pedal bin, lid yawning open with empty pot noodle containers and chip papers, and turned the pages.

Hold on! What am I doing? I haven't got time for this, have I?

He slammed the album shut, reached for his bag, dug out

his switch, looped it around his neck and rummaged through the kitchen drawers until he found a pair of scissors. He ran upstairs, dragged his old padded jacket from his wardrobe, pulled it on and studied himself in the wardrobe mirror. Neat. With the zip done up the switch was hardly noticeable underneath. He delved into the pockets: three shrivelled conkers, his missing glove, a fifty pence piece, a toffee stuck to a bus ticket, two Mars Bar wrappers and – *that's* where his Walkman headphones had got to. He threw them on the bed.

He tugged out the pocket linings, snipped off the bottoms with the scissors and stuffed them back inside. Perfect. His hands rested comfortably on the box. He groped carefully for the button and the switch. To anyone else he was just a boy with his hands in his pockets. A slightly tubby one, that's all. He didn't want any awkward questions. He'd look daft enough staring into space, but with a box of dials hanging round his waist it was asking for trouble.

He checked his watch. Only ten to four. Loads of time. Look out Normans. Nathan the Saxon's coming.

He ran downstairs to the front door, stopped, ran back and scribbled a note.

> *Dear Dad*
> *I'm back. Got loads of homework. Gone to do some*
> *historical research. Home for tea.*
> > *Love Nathe*
> *P.S. I hate pot noodles.*
> *P.P.S. I think I'm going off chips.*

*

Nathan stood on the corner by Lloyds Bank and stared up at the castle on its mound high above him. Its squared battlements and massive walls dominated the marketplace and streets below. Its slitted windows peered darkly at him from beneath curved arches.

Wow! Menacing.

He'd never really looked at it properly before. Till now, it was just – there. Even the late afternoon sunshine which had turned the stone walls to the colour of honey, could not soften its looming presence.

Now think, Nathe. What did Mr Onslow say about the castle? The Normans built a wooden one first, didn't they? Sometime around 1068. And they were in a hurry, needed to take control quickly. A fortress where they could garrison their army and watch the wily and rebellious Saxons. Not bad, Nathe. Old Onslow'd be well impressed. Better get a bit closer – how about near the steps? Now set the time dials for 1068. The rest'll have to be hit and miss.

An hour and a half later Nathan was coming to the conclusion that he was going to have to do his homework without the help of the switch. He'd tried everywhere he could think of. The front, back and sides of the castle, the bridge, the path – nothing, except earache from the swooping hum of the switch.

"Useless. Blooming useless," he told a small girl licking an ice-cream and staring up at him with interest. She ran off to her mum.

And why, today of all days, does it have to be so

77

blooming hot? I think I may be melting inside this jacket. Hang about! What about trying inside the castle? It'll be cooler there.

Adults: £1.80. Children under twelve: 70p, said the notice on the wall.

He searched his trouser pockets. 9p. Not even enough for a lolly. He could do with one right now. He trudged down the steps, climbed across to the slope of the mound and threw himself onto the grass. He unzipped his coat and rolled onto his front. That was better.

No one about. Give it one more go. He pressed the switch's button. He knew instantly.

It's working! It's working! We have a switch.

I'm shouting. Strange words. Foreign-sounding words. But I understand everything I'm saying. Shouting above the din: children crying, shouts, screams, sounds of things being smashed and broken. It's drizzling with rain. I'm giving orders – to men wearing helmets and chain mail – rough-shaven, swords at the ready, axes hanging from their belts. Boy, they're fearsome! They're Normans, aren't they? Norman soldiers. I wouldn't want to get on the wrong side of *them*. They're looking up at me – listening to every word I say. I'm sitting, sitting astride a horse. It's huge! The ground's miles away. I hope I know how to control this thing. It's restless. I tug the reins with a thick, hairy hand. Me! The closest thing I ever got to a horse was a donkey ride on the beach. I must be a Norman knight or something.

"Burn every building still standing. If they won't come out, set fire to the thatch," I order, pointing. "I want the area cleared before dark. No idlers. Anyone who can stand digs. Do it.

"There'll be rewards for those who deserve it!" I call after them.

They run towards the houses.

I'm on a sort of earth bank, looking down. People everywhere, bodies on the ground where they've fallen – there's things here I don't want to look at. Groups being herded along by soldiers. Others huddling together. A small child standing alone. Men being separated from the women and children. Pigs and hens, squawking and grunting as soldiers try to catch them. And the smells. Smoke – choking smoke – from blackened and burning buildings. And wet earth, and animal smells. Mud everywhere. I'm tugging the horse round, behind me a deep black earthy ditch. People digging – men and women and children, bent over, covered in dirt and mud, like burrowing black beatles. A soldier kicks at a boy who stops to rest. Men dragging carts of earth up a bank, struggling on all fours on the slippery mud . . .

They're building the mound – that's what they're doing! The mound for the castle.

More people being herded by a soldier towards another shallow ditch. He points and barks orders. They don't understand. A woman with a baby in her arms and a little girl. I'm shouting an order at the soldier. I tell him to – this is terrible, how can I do this? The soldier listens and obeys. He's snatching the baby – and tossing it into the ditch. The

79

woman screams, leaps after it, slithering down the muddy slope. It's OK, I think. She's picking it up, it stops crying. The soldier throws down shovels and points. Everyone gets the message. They scramble into the ditch and start digging. I am definitely *not* a very nice person.

I sit here watching. I'm smiling. I feel so – powerful. I see some soldiers coming out of a house, carrying bundles. I shout and beckon them over – they've found some rolls of cloth – and some silver plate. I order them to set it aside for me. If they serve me well, I'm promising, this will be shared out.

More crashing sounds, soldiers breaking into a house. Screams from inside another that explodes into flames as the thatch catches.

A sudden shout. I'm turning to see – a man running. I kick my horse and give chase. I'm laughing, I'm enjoying this – how can I? Starting to fade as I catch him up. The glimpse of a pale face staring up at me, terrified eyes. I strike downwards – the glint of metal – red . . .

I can't watch!

Nathan squeezed his eyes shut. His hands flew up to his head as he let go of the switch.

"So I told him what he could do with his job," said a voice below him.

Nathan blinked back into the twentieth century. There was no decapitated head on the grass below him. Just two women, their backs to him, chatting on the bench on the path.

80

So it wasn't me screaming then? They'd be staring up, wouldn't they, if it had been me? I'll never forget that scream. It was terrible.

He slowly scanned his surroundings; the neat flowerbeds, the litter bins, the grassy slopes. No screaming and shouting. Just the hum of traffic and the twittering of birds. He could see now why it had been so difficult to switch. It was pure luck he'd managed to switch at all.

Yeah – the ground levels are different, aren't they? The top of the mound didn't exist in ...

He checked the dials.

25 April 1068. Old Onslow was right. The Normans smashed the Saxon town and used the people as slave labour – digging the ditches, and using the earth to build the surrounding defences and the mound for the castle. I must have caught the start of it all. All I've got to do now is fast forward and – *kerpow!* – the castle will be there.

He peered up at the castle.

It's still here. All those hundreds of years and it's still here. And this mound – I saw them build it. Am I glad I wasn't around then. Do people here realise just what went into this mound? There ought to be a monument to all those poor Saxons.

He stared down at his sword arm, half expecting to see it covered in blood. He shivered at the memory.

I don't think I want to be a Saxon right now. I'll be a Saxon tomorrow. A nice obedient Saxon who doesn't get his head lopped off. Don't fancy all that digging though. I'll never forget that scream.

"Sorry, Dad, got delayed," panted Nathan.

He'd lost track of time in the Castle Gardens and had to run all the way home.

"Twenty to seven, Nathan," grumbled Dad, tapping his watch. "Where have you been? I was expecting you three quarters of an hour ago. Had to stick the dinner in the oven to keep warm – probably spoiled by now. Aren't you a bit hot with that coat zipped up?"

I got delayed in 1068, Dad, he wanted to shout. I've been a Norman knight, conquering the Saxons! Time flies when you're busy. Nine hundred years just whizzed by.

What he actually said was, "I'll just go and change then."

He ripped off his coat, hid his switch in a drawer and peeled off his sticky T-shirt.

A bit whiffy.

He dashed into the bathroom, sprinkled himself liberally with some of Mum's old talcum powder, and searched for a clean T-shirt.

"Hurry up!" called Dad. "It's ready."

"Special tonight," said Dad, gathering up the takeaway containers. The pink clothes had vanished. So had the aroma of smelly dog. Something lemony hung heavy in the air. Two places had been set on the kitchen table.

"Yeah!" agreed Nathan. "Fave, Dad. Chicken tikka and nan bread."

"Let's tuck in then," said Dad, looking immensely pleased with himself.

The phone rang just as Dad was serving up the ice-cream.

"Hello," said Dad. "Yes. He's here. No need to raise your voice. It's none of my doing. He's a free agent, you know."

He held out the phone to Nathan. "Your mother. She wants to speak to *you*."

Nathan half rose from his chair, then sat down again.

"Tell her I'm busy," he said with a mouthful of ice-cream.

"He says he's busy," said Dad to the phone.

"She says do you know how worried she's been?" said Dad.

Nathan frowned thoughtfully.

"Can't this wait? He's eating his dinner," Dad said to the phone.

"She says why didn't you tell her you weren't coming home?"

"I am home," said Nathan.

Dad smiled.

"He says he *is* home," said Dad. Dad winked at him as he said it.

"She says what's she supposed to do with the chicken" – he was laughing – "the chicken tikka she bought specially?"

"Tell her to give it to Smelly Mike."

"He says— Hello?" Dad held out the phone, looked at it and hung up. "She put the phone down," he said.

"Good to have you back, Nathe," said Dad, ruffling Nathan's hair and helping himself to ice-cream. "Smelly Mike, eh? One of those students, is he?"

"Mmm," said Nathan. "This ice-cream is yum."

"Nothing but the best, Nathan," said Dad. "Now what's this homework you've got? I can give you a hand. I used to like history."

"A day in the life of a Saxon," mumbled Nathan.

"That's the sort of thing they get you to do these days, is it?" said Dad leaning back in his chair. "What about dates? That's what's important. I hope you know your dates . . ."

"Battle of Hastings, 1066," boasted Nathan.

"Everyone knows that," said Dad. "But when was Magna Carta, eh? Tell me that?"

"We haven't done that yet, Dad."

"Twelve fifteen," said Dad.

"Henry the Eighth's six wives, done that yet?"

"No, Dad."

"Well you just ask if you need any help, eh?"

"Yes, Dad. Thanks, Dad."

"Been a bit difficult then, has she — your mother?" said Dad as they cleared the table. "What's the problem exactly, Nathan?"

"I just needed some more space, Dad. Like you said, I've got to think of my school work."

Dad nodded.

"Well, you're here now, eh? What's she doing these days, then?"

Here we go again, thought Nathan. The interrogation. What's she doing, where's she been, what she said. Nathan the Undercover Agent. I don't think you'd want to know, Dad.

"Learning to drive," said Nathan.

"Ha!" said Dad. "Well, glad it's not *my* car, eh, Nathe? D'you remember that time—"

"Crumbs! Is that the time?" said Nathan, looking at his watch. "Sorry, Dad, I've got to go. Promised Gav I'd call round."

"But I thought we might have a game – Ludo or something. You used to like that."

"When I was six or something, Dad."

Dad had the expression of a small boy who'd just discovered no one had remembered his birthday.

"All right. When I get back then," said Nathan.

"Hello, Nathan," said Gav's mum as she opened the door with an armful of pillows. "Gavin's out, I'm afraid. Just popped down to Tesco's for me. Should be back soon though."

"Stick them up," said Gav's little brother, peering round the doorway with a water pistol.

"Mum! Where's my snorkel?" shouted Gav's sister from over the hall banister.

"On top of the microwave," shouted Gav's mum.

"We're taking the caravan down to Bournemouth for the weekend," said Gav's mum. "Seeing as it's turned out so nice."

"Jeff?" called Gav's mum. "Put these in the van for me, will you?"

"Hello, Nathan," said Gav's dad, leaning out from the caravan parked in the drive and taking the pillows. "All right, then?"

"Yeah, thanks," said Nathan. "Tell Gav – it doesn't matter – I'll see him on Monday."

"Have you got the toilet rolls?" shouted Gav's mum to the van.

"Have a nice time," mumbled Nathan.

Nathan felt too restless to return to Dad's. He mooched around for a while. He tugged the drawers on the chocolate machines outside Ferris's. He checked the hole in the wall at Barclays Bank just in case someone had been absent-minded enough to leave behind a wad of ten pound notes. He scrutinised the video games in the window of One Step Beyond. He returned to the Castle Gardens and replayed the Norman knight experience in his head for the hundredth time. He caught thirteen gnats. He dawdled back to Bryjan.

Oh no. Who's this heading towards me? Not Nina Nicholson. Yes. Nina Nicholson. Best friend of Tansy. Both members of the charisma award committee. Pretend you haven't seen her. Cross over. Real casual. Mmmm. That gutter's very interesting. Keep your eyes on the gutter, Nathe.

"Hi, Nathe!"

Heck. She's crossing over.

He could feel the pink creeping up his neck to his face.

Think white. Think ice. Think cool. Cool white ice.

"You still live round here then, Nathe? I thought you'd moved."

"Yeah, well, sometimes. Like, my dad's still here but my mum's moved."

She nodded. "Yeah. My dad left when I was little. He's in Coventry now."

"Right," said Nathan. "Well . . ."

"We were only joking you know."

"What?"

"In the playground the other day – about charisma – we were only having a laugh."

"Oh, *that*. I'd forgotten about that."

He stuffed his hands in his pockets. And missed. They dangled hugely by his sides. Had his hands always been this big? Had they always twitched like this? They seemed to have a life of their own.

"You were dead funny in Maths today," she grinned.

He felt carefully for his pockets and tried again; a surge of relief as his hands slid into them.

"I told my mum what you said. She laughed her head off."

"Yeah?" he shrugged modestly.

"You growing your hair?" she asked, peering at his neck.

"No," said Nathan, testing the back of his head with his hand just in case it had spontaneously sprouted several inches without his noticing.

"Yeah – it's definitely longer. It suits you."

"Yeah?"

He kicked at the manhole cover.

"You've got really nice hair. Your mum's got nice hair, hasn't she? Bit darker than yours and wavy. I wish I had nice hair."

She was waiting for him to say something.

"You've got nice hair," he said.

"No, it's horrible – brown and straight."

"No, it's nice."

"Really?"

"Yeah. It's brown and straight and – nice."

She smiled. Now she was going pink.

"Well – be seeing you – got to go – I'm late – meeting Tansy."

She ran off.

Yeah. She's all right is Nina. Even though she hit me with a toy frying pan that time in the Wendy house in the infants because I wouldn't eat the pretend scrambled eggs she'd cooked.

He ran round the corner, leapt onto the up-and-down wall that ran outside the parade of shops, jogged home, vaulted Bryjan's gate, ran through the back door and up to his room.

"Nathan? Is that you?" called Dad.

"Yeah – down in a sec."

He examined himself in the mirror, tugging at the hair at the nape of his neck to make it grow. Nice hair. Titian. Not carrot, or ginger, or rusty or tango. Nice.

"You've got really nice hair, Nathe," he told his reflection.

He breathed onto the glass and with a finger wrote:

KARISMA

8
~
Back Again
~

Nathan set off at a quarter to eight the next morning. On a Saturday the town would soon be busy with shoppers and tourists. He wanted an early start.

The sky was a clear blue. He was glad he'd abandoned his thick jacket. All the signs said it was going to be a hot day. Instead he wore his new baggy shirt.

Just don't let Mum get her hands on it. She'll go mental if she sees what I've done with the pockets. Right – where to start then? Give the castle a wide berth today, I think. Don't fancy being a Saxon slave.

He paused for a moment and tried to visualise the worksheet he'd filled in showing the layout of the old town. Where was the Saxon marketplace? Somewhere near East-gate Street, wasn't it?

He set off again.

Right. Here we are then. Shops not even open yet. No one about. Let's try 1069 – how about July? He pulled up his shirt, set the time dials, switched on, tugged down his shirt and pressed the button. I don't believe it! First time! I'm switching – here we go ...

Phfaw! The stink!

His finger came off the button as his head reeled and he switched back to himself. It struck him suddenly that the button was a very useful feature of the switch. In moments of horror – or terrible smells – it was an automatic reaction to let go. A sort of safety device: when you didn't have time, or the presence of mind to find the switch and flick it off.

Yeah – without the button, things could be seriously deadly. I mean – what if by chance I'd switched to that poor Saxon who lost his head? What would have happened to the real me? I might have died from shock, mightn't I? Right, nostrils, are you ready? Here we go again . . .

Yuk. It's fish, isn't it? Mixed up with a few things I'd rather not think about. Very smelly times, these. I can see the fish now – and some crabs – and shellfish – all in boxes and baskets set out on the ground.

"Fish, fresh fish!" I'm shouting in a shrill voice. "Nothing so nice and cheap at the price! What better dish than a nice piece of fish!"

Crowds of people. Stalls and tables – I'm serving a woman in a brown dress – she picks up a crab, puts it in her basket and hands me some coins. I slip them into a leather purse round my waist. Bending down now – counting how many fish left – wearing a long greyish skirt and sort of wooden shoes. As I straighten up I can see I'm right in the middle of the market. There's vegetables and chickens and pots and leather things – and all the time I'm calling, "Fish, fresh fish . . ."

A big cheer goes up – turning to look – there's an open space where a crowd's watching a man juggling. A small boy coming on, climbing onto his shoulders – leaps – somersaults and lands on his feet. He picks up the coins that have been thrown down — tosses them up and catches them in his mouth — hasn't he heard of *germs*? What's happening? The boy and the juggler suddenly disappear — it's gone quiet — people stepping back — some soldiers swaggering through — stopping at a stall where a girl is selling cherries — talking to her — bellowing with laughter. They move on — eating cherries. The girl spits after them as they leave.

"I'd like to give them something," I'm muttering to an old man. "Poison!"

"Poison's too good for them," says the man.

Nathan sat on the wall, licking his lolly. He didn't hear the traffic or the busker on the corner or see the shoppers. Strange words echoed in his head; words he used when he'd switched but which now had no meaning. His head was crammed with images he couldn't switch off. The legless man begging. The blind girl with the twisted face scrounging from the market stalls.

He'd got the bearing of the Saxon town now. Felt as if he lived there. He'd fast forwarded and watched the castle grow from its simple wooden tower on the mound to a vast fortress; its thick stone walls rising above the town. Watched it sprawl like a monster in its lair, surrounded by its great steep earthbanks topped with wooden palisades, its network of ditches and gatehouses. It loomed above them, watching their every move, waiting to devour them.

"Excuse me, we're looking for the castle."

A man with a camera slung around his neck, a woman and a bored-looking girl waited for an answer. He gave them directions and they set off. He was bursting to tell them everything he'd seen, stand on the wall and yell it out to all the passers-by who scurried past with their bags and their crying children and their shopping lists.

Look — see where that dog's sniffing, he wanted to shout, *an old Saxon woman used to sell fish there!*

They'd put you away, Nathe.

And how am I going to write this all down? I've got enough for a book here. I've switched into so many different people — men, women, children, that poor kid with the terrible cough. And it's all so mixed up. Like when I'm a Saxon and see what the Normans are doing, the way they treat us — those public punishments and executions. I had to switch off then. And the way they just take everything they want — well — I hate them so much it *hurts*. I just want to kill them. But when I'm a Norman — well — it all seems to make sense. I'm thinking, If they can't defend themselves, it's winner takes all, isn't it? If a few thousand of us can walk in and take over, they deserve everything they've got coming. They can learn a lot from us. You've got to be hard — show them you mean business.

I've got enough for a whole chapter on old William the Conqueror. I mean — how many people can say they've actually *seen* William the Conqueror? Not what I imagined at all. Quite old. Stubby little legs. And the haircut — shaved halfway up the back of his head, all bushy on top, like he's wearing a wig and it's tipped forward. It's how all the Normans wear it. But it's his eyes you notice first — piercing pale blue — like they can see right through you. I saw him really close up, surrounded by his bodyguard on their way to the castle. He was laughing. Terrible teeth though. And kept putting his tongue in his cheek. One of the guards said he had toothache something awful. Now you don't get that in history books, do you?

"So this is where you're hiding."

"I'm not hiding," said Nathan, rolling over on his bed. "You were out when I got back."

He'd been trying to draw William the Conqueror as he remembered him, before the tiredness that seemed to follow switching overtook him.

"Library, was it?" said Dad.

"What?"

"Your research – history homework."

"Oh – that's right," Nathan nodded.

Well, he had actually gone into the library, hadn't he? For about two minutes, when he thought he'd seen Nina go in. He'd hoped she might appreciate a few tips on the Saxon experience. But it hadn't been Nina after all.

"I've been shopping," Dad announced importantly.

"Well done, Dad."

"Come and see what I've bought then."

"Dad, I'm not really that interested in the contents of a Sainsbury's bag."

"Who said anything about Sainsbury's?" said Dad mysteriously and disappeared from the doorway.

Nathan followed.

"What d'you think then, Nathan?" said Dad.

There was a shiny black rectangular thing on the sitting-room carpet.

"What is it?" said Nathan.

"What is it?" repeated Dad. "I'll tell you what this is, Nathan. This is a new video recorder."

"But we've got one, Dad."

"Not like this, Nathan. This is a state-of-the-art video. See this? This is TM easy programming. Just tap in the code of the programme you want to record – and Bob's your uncle. Stereo sound, picture search, indexing, screen graphics – good, eh?"

"Excellent, Dad," said Nathan, kneeling down to examine it.

"It's yours, Nathan," said Dad.

"What?"

"It's yours. I bought it for you. A present."

"Wow! Thanks, Dad. It's brill."

"Now, let's set it up. Tell you what, Nathan, while I'm doing this . . ."

He reached into his back pocket and counted out three new ten-pound notes.

". . . go and buy yourself some videos, eh?"

"Cor, thanks, Dad!"

Dad had a pizza for him when he got back. But he'd only had a couple of bites before sleep won the battle to keep his eyes open. Dad said he thought *The Simpsons* video was a waste of money. Nathan couldn't argue. He'd slept all the way through it.

*

94

Nathan threw down his pen and slumped across the table.

"Boy's hand falls off after seven-hour homework stint," he groaned.

All day Sunday it had taken.

But I've done it, haven't I? Feel much better now that it's all down on paper, let it all out. And not fifteen lines but fifteen pages. Without the biscuit crumbs. Didn't help having Dad constantly trying to be helpful though.

"What's this word meant to be, Nathan?"

"Is this handwriting the best you can do? You're not giving it in like this are you?"

"Don't they teach you punctuation these days, then?"

"It's only a rough draft, Dad."

"Rough draft? Wouldn't have got away with that in my day."

"Thanks, Dad."

He sat up. He could hear a whirring come from above his head. Come to think of it, there'd been a lot of whirring for the last hour or so.

Better start packing up then. Got to face Mum now. Don't think about it.

He made his way upstairs to his room.

"*Dee-dah!*" sang Dad as Nathan stepped across the threshold.

A new shelf jutted proudly from the wall.

"Oh – excell*ent*," said Nathan.

Plan E in operation. All systems go. Can't remember when Dad's been so normal.

Nathan moved his stuffed stoat onto the new shelf to

show his appreciation. He started to pack his school uniform into his holdall.

"What you doing, Nathan?" said Dad.

"Got to go now, Dad."

"Go? Go where?"

"Back to Mum's of course," said Nathan, shoving in his blazer. "Dad, can you see my other sock anywhere? She goes bananas – what's the matter, Dad?"

"But you said you'd come back," said Dad very quietly.

"Only for the weekend, Dad."

Dad stood there clutching his screwdriver, an intense look on his face as if the words Nathan had just spoken had gone into slow motion and hadn't quite reached him yet.

Oh dear. What have you done, Nathe? *That's* why Dad was in such a good mood. Look what you've done, Nathe.

"That's not what you said, Nathan. 'I'm back' your note said. 'This is my home.' That's what you said. What are you playing at, Nathan?"

"I dunno. I didn't mean—"

"Well, that makes it all right then," said Dad. "You didn't mean it – fine. Go on then – pack your bags."

He gave a long sigh and tossed his screwdriver into his toolbag.

"I should be used to this by now, shouldn't I?"

"I've *got* to go, Dad," said Nathan.

"Don't bother trying to explain – I've heard all this before—"

"No, Dad, you don't understand . . ."

"Oh yes, I understand perfectly," said Dad.

"But, Dad ..."

"I think I've heard all I want to hear, thank you," said Dad.

"Dad — just listen!" Nathan shouted.

"Don't shout, Nathan."

"Listen, Dad!" shouted Nathan. "It's because of Smelly Mike. He's — he's Mum's new boyfriend! He's why I've got to go back!"

Nathan told him everything. Like how slimy he was. Like how worried sick he'd been when Mum didn't come home. How Mum had wanted *him* to apologise to Mike. He added a nose stud and some lurid tattoos.

Dad was staring at him. "Let's get this straight, Nathan," he said, pushing back his hair. "She brought this Mike back to the flat? And she didn't get back to *what* time?"

Dad marched downstairs. Nathan followed.

I don't think you should have said all that, Nathe.

Dad had the phone in his hand and was dialling.

"Before you put the phone down, Janice," he said quietly, "you'd better listen very carefully ..."

He spoke every word with clipped precision.

"... because if you don't I'll be round there personally. Nathan has just told me ..."

Nathan winced at the mention of his name.

Long pause now as Dad listened, tapping the wall with his fingers.

"Oh yes it is! It's very much my business! He's my son too just in case you'd forgotten ..."

Nathan covered his ears.

"... enough damage without ..."

"Oh, Dad," groaned Nathan.

"There's no point in shouting! Here we go – into emotional overdrive. This is just typical – you never could take criticism ..."

"Dad ..." said Nathan.

Dad waved him away.

"It's totally irresponsible. I'm warning you, Janice, if ..."

Nathan went and sat on the stairs.

Dad was sitting at the kitchen table, staring at the spoon he was turning over and over between his fingers.

I shouldn't have told him about Mum and Mike. Look at him. He's really moody now. Back down in the dumps. Just when he was cheering up, too. Why couldn't I keep my lip zipped?

His hair was sticking up from where he kept running his hand through it. His shirt was straining at the buttons as he leaned forward. One button had popped off.

"I told your mother what I think of her behaviour," said Dad. "You're probably right – best you get back. Keep an eye on things. Let me know if there's any more trouble. Especially with this Mike. I don't like the sound of him at all. If it happens again, I want to know about it, right? Straight away."

"Right," sighed Nathan. Nathan the Spy.

Oh, Dad, thought Nathan. Did you have to? Mum'll be cyclonic now. Why did I have to open my mouth? Dad, this isn't the way to get Mum back. Mum's right. You're making things worse.

"I'll just clean up, then," said Dad, heaving himself up. "Then I'll run you back."

"No, it's OK, Dad . . ."

"I'll run you back, Nathan," said Dad.

Well done, Nathe. You handled that really well. You've really stirred things up now.

Nathan trudged upstairs to fetch his things. He sat on his bed and dragged his bag towards him.

Plan E.

Result: Failure. Completely down the drain. Pull the chain.

I'm not sure I can help you any more, Dad. I've run out of ideas. You're hard work, Dad, when you're like this. Not sure I can take any more. Not that you haven't got your good points. Like – well – let's think:

A whizz with the old Black and Decker. Used to be.

Can cover nought to five mph with the hover mower. Used to.

Can repair a flat tyre in under sixty seconds. Well, before my bike got nicked.

The only person who could get Nan's cat, Tiger, to take his worm tablets. Before he went to cat heaven.

Complete recall of all matches played by Liverpool Football Club, and . . .

Reliable. *Very* reliable.

But it's not enough, is it? It's not going to get Mum banging on the front door demanding to be let in. Not even if I drop a few reminders and do a big promotion job. Yeah. You've really done it now, Dad. Ably assisted by your son and heir. We've blown it, Dad.

Nathan reached for his pillow and hit himself over the head several times.

"Stupid! Stupid! Stupid!" he groaned.

The word KARISMA glimmered faintly in the glass of his wardrobe mirror. He levered himself off the bed and stood before it.

"Charisma," he mouthed.

You must have had a bit once, Dad. Whatever Mum says now. She's just not telling. Or she's forgotten. Where'd it go, Dad? 'Cos, quite frankly, I've got to tell you, I've not seen much evidence of it myself lately. Like last week when I dropped in, I couldn't help noticing you had a dried pot noodle stuck to your chin. Chow Mein flavour, if I'm not mistaken. And those crisp crumbs on your jumper didn't do a lot for you either. And have you seen your feet lately, Dad? Must be quite difficult with that – excuse the word – large *belly* of yours. I think it might be something to do with all those chips, Dad. And Friday night, Dad, blaming the chicken tikka for that burping episode. Well, Dad, it's all a bit off-putting, if you want the truth.

"I'll wait for you in the car," called Dad.

Nathan hoisted his bags onto his shoulder and plodded downstairs. He was halfway out of the front door when he remembered.

Homework, Nathe! You forgot your homework!

He gathered it up from the table and rolled it into a tube. The car hooter honked. Nathan put the tube to his eye, like a telescope and peered through it out of the window. Framed in its circular opening, he could see Dad sitting in the car, tapping the wheel impatiently. As he swung it down, his eye caught something he'd seen so many times he'd never really noticed it. On the window ledge, alongside the school photos of himself, was Mum and Dad's wedding photo. Bending low and stepping forward, he zoomed in on it. Just the two of them, standing in a church doorway, Mum in her frilly dress, Dad, slim, in a white suit. She, gazing up at Dad, Dad smiling down at her.

Look at the way she's looking at you, Dad. You definitely had something once. Whatever it was, you lost it, Dad. Be nice if she looked at you like that now.

He moved his telescope to the left. Another photo. Mum and Dad holding up a tiny, sleepy baby.

Cor – you were dead ugly, Nathe.

The car hooted again. He ran out and slammed the door.

Dad was sitting in the car, head lolling back, staring up at nothing. He was wearing one of his pink T-shirts. It had shrunk.

"Took your time," said Dad.

As Dad turned the ignition key, a spark of an idea flashed inside Nathan's head. It flickered into life, then filled him with a dazzling glow.

It's brilliant! Totally brilliant!

Plan F: *THE QUEST FOR DAD'S LOST CHARISMA*

ACTION: Nathan, the seeker of charisma, with the aid of

101

his faithful switch, will search for it, find it and restore it to its rightful owner.

AIM: Make Mum fall in love with Dad again.

It's simple! All I've got to do is switch back into Mum, find out what Dad once had that's gone missing, and help him put it back! Mum won't know what's hit her. History will repeat itself. It'll be like meeting Dad for the first time, all over again. If it worked the first time, it'll work again!

Dad pulled up outside Mum's place.

"That's not his car is it?" he asked, nodding to a BMW.

It was the first thing he'd said since setting off.

"No. He's got an XR3," said Nathan.

Dad sniffed and stared out of the window.

"Let me know if you have any trouble with this Mike," said Dad. "I'll be seeing you soon, I hope. If you can spare the time."

"Yeah – all right. Thanks for the video!" he called as Dad drove off.

He watched Dad's car turn the corner, then stepped back to look up at the window of Mum's flat. He let out a long sigh, like an escaping ghost.

Another week with Dad in zombie mode then. And now Mum to face. Given the choice between Mum and the Normans right now, I think I'd take my chances with the Normans. Battle-axes and all.

He pushed open the street door.

Just think of Plan F, Nathe. It's going to work this time. You're going to *make* it work, Nathe. Nathan the Invincible.

102

9

~

What Are You Playing At?

~

Nathan slid his key into the lock of Mum's flat, gently turned it, carefully edged the door open, crept in and slowly, painstakingly, eased it shut.

The room was dim, the only light coming from the television in the corner. He could see Mum's bare feet propped up on the sofa arm. The rest of her was hidden by the back of the sofa.

He didn't know what to do next. He stood, trying to keep still and not to breathe too loudly, wondering why Mum couldn't hear his heart pounding. It was thumping away like a demented drummer. He wished he'd brought a white flag with him.

What you gonna say, Nathe?

Hi, Mum! Long time no see. Fancy seeing you . . . *Reject*.

Dad kidnapped me, Mum. I had to break the window and . . . *Reject*.

Oh, help someone! Come on, Nathe, think of something. I know – I'll go for a long walk and . . .

He took a cautious step backwards and stumbled.

"AAAAAAAGH!"

The scream came from Mum. She was standing, leaning against the sofa, hand pressed to her chest, heaving and gasping.

"God, Nathan," she panted, "what – what are you –

playing at! I thought – don't – ever – do that – again, Nathan!"

She dropped onto the sofa arm, taking deep breaths. Then she looked up at him. "You've got a nerve, Nathan," she said very quietly, glaring through narrow eyes.

Why wasn't she shouting at him? This made him feel worse.

"Creeping back, after all you've done."

She was in her dressing gown, her hair was falling down, her eyes red and puffy. She threw up her hands as if tossing confetti and looked away.

"I don't know what to say, Nathan, if you want the truth. How could you? Eh? You might have at least told me you were going to your dad's. Why didn't you *tell* me? Or leave a note? Not too much trouble, is it? But that's nothing, Nathan – compared to the other thing."

She flicked her hair from her eyes.

"Sneaky, that's the word, Nathan. Sneaky. Lies – most of it. What were you trying to do, for goodness sakes?"

She waved her hands as if pushing him away, flopped forward, stared down at her feet.

"I'd never have believed it of you, Nathan," she said without looking up.

"Why?" She shrugged. "You of all people. That's what *really* hurts. I didn't think things could get much worse between me and your father – but you've managed it, Nathan. Oh yes. You certainly managed it."

She looked up. Her eyes were watery. She glanced down at his bags, then away.

Nathan drooped like a puppet with loose strings. He stared down at his trailing lace. Squeezed his eyes hard to stop them doing something embarrassing. Slowly he bent down and picked up his bags, turned for the door, reached for the handle.

"Oh, Nathe! Come here."

And then she was all over him. Her hair kept getting in his mouth. He tried to spit it out. He wanted to howl. He bit his lip, concentrated on the butterfly pattern of Mum's dressing gown: cabbage white, buttercup yellow, red admiral, leaf green . . .

"I'm sorry, Mum—"

He couldn't finish the rest.

"Come on," said Mum, "let's sit down, eh?"

Nathan stood stiffly, a bag in each hand, as she tugged him.

"What's the matter, Nathe?"

"I feel soppy."

"Soppy's good for you sometimes, Nathe. And I'm in a soppy mood."

They sat on the sofa together.

"Truce, Nathe?" said Mum.

"Truce," said Nathan.

She made him hot chocolate. They watched television. And all the time, he kept thinking of Dad.

Nathan the Traitor: 2

On Monday morning, Nathan woke up in Mum's room. She'd swapped with him for the sofa bed.

"I've been thinking about it for a while," she said. "It makes sense considering I'm up first and last to bed. Perhaps later, when I've got a bit more money coming in, I can find a flat with more space. You need a room of your own, Nathe and – oh, I haven't told you, have I? – about those Pot Peru pots? Brindles have put in an order. There's going to be a special feature in the *Advertiser*."

Nathan was only half listening. He was scanning the flat for clues to the Smelly Mike Conquest. Someone had made a one coffee-mug phone call, that was all. No sign of the enemy.

"Oh, yeah, Mum. You've got to sign something for school."

"Can't it wait, Nathe. I'll be late."

He dangled the two detention slips.

"One today, one on Friday. I'll get another if I don't get them signed."

"Nathan – this is terrible. Two? Why?"

She peered at them.

"Time-wasting and not paying attention – and two entries in the Late Book – oh, Nathe."

"Not my fault if I'm tired, is it? Staying up late – waiting for people . . ."

"I thought we had a truce, Nathe," said Mum, scribbling her signature on the dotted lines.

So – the weekend hasn't been a *complete* disaster, Nathan decided as he set off for school.

Cheer up, Nathe. Everyone wants to give you things: a

106

new video machine and your own room. You've got Plan F all waiting to go – *and* you finished your history homework. Can't be bad, can it? Whatever the dreaded red pen scrawls this time, it can't complain about the quantity.

Nathan had numbered each page with day-glo green explosions, just in case Mr Onslow didn't notice how many there were.

Yeah, I probably know more about the Saxons and the Normans, than old Onslow now. Nathan the Saxon Expert. *And* I found my headphones, didn't I?

He slipped them onto his head, plugged them into his Walkman, switched on, and, head nodding to the beat, walked to school.

"It was brilliant," Gav was telling him. "I went snorkelling at this place called Man-o'-War Bay – you could see right down . . ."

They were in the music studio, waiting for Miss Dickenson to turn up for the lesson. She was already five minutes late.

A paper dart flew past his ear and landed on the floor next to Kevin who was being stupid with a ruler. Nathan bent to pick it up but somehow his fingers missed and Neil beat him to it. Then he saw Nina on the other side of the room, trying to tell him something.

"What?" he mouthed back.

". . . and then on Sunday Dad took us to . . ." Gav was shouting.

Nathan reached into his bag, stood up and walked to the front of the class.

"Where you going?" called Gav.

Nathan stopped by the tape deck, peered at it, switched on, slipped in a cassette tape and pressed Play.

A sudden burst of sound made heads turn.

"What's that?" said someone.

The chords of a guitar rippled from the speakers.

"Turn it down," said another.

"No, it's good. Listen!" someone shouted.

A harsh beat was stabbing beneath the guitar now.

"You'll get us all into trouble," moaned someone else.

The beat was faster, tighter now, insistent. Now a voice began to sing.

"Hey, listen, it's about school or something!" shouted Steven.

The voice was rising and falling. Then voice, guitar, the throbbing beat meshed together in a whole wall of sound.

A screech of brakes.

The heavy throb of the guitar again . . .

"Nathan jumped onto the teacher's table at the front of the room.

"What's he doing? He's gone mad."

"*We don't need no education*," sang the voice.

The air filled with the stabbing beat and the words.

"*We don't need no thought control*."

Heads were nodding now – they couldn't help it.

Suddenly, Nina jumped up onto her table, then Tansy and Steven. Others copied – some not sure – checking the door to see if Miss Dickenson had come in. A few more jumped up.

"*Hey! Teacher! Leave us kids alone!*" it sang.

More than half the class were on their tables now. Swaying and stamping in time to the beat, punching the air with their fists.

"*All in all – you're just another brick in the wall!*"

"Turn it up, turn it up!" they shouted.

They were all up now. Even Malcolm Hetherington, whose favourite motto was "Why don't you just grow up?", was stomping and swaying with the rest. He'd even undone his blazer. The whole class, swaying from side to side like a great navy blue sea, arms reaching for and stabbing at the ceiling.

It was the chorus of kids' voices now, repeating the words, like a chant, "*We don't need no education,*" and the whole class was singing and swaying. Some of the girls were doing their own thing – choreographing with their hands and arms as if building a wall, brick by brick, trying to peer over the top.

The guitar solo soared and rippled, sang its notes …

Nathan clutched his invisible guitar, skilfully played the strings, crouched over it, fingers working the chords.

Others started to copy. The class, an orchestra of invisible guitars, throbbing and strumming, plucking their strings with nimble fingers.

Bodies swayed or crouched over their guitars. Feet stomped. Their voices as one:

"*All in all – you're just another brick in the wall!*"

As it faded away, those who still had their eyes closed in hypnotised concentration were the last to observe that Miss Dickenson had entered the room. One or two had instantly jumped down and were now pretending to be reading. One by one, the gyrations and the stomping ground to a halt.

"Stay exactly where you are," she ordered.

She walked slowly to the front of the room, switched off the music and removed the tape. Nathan shrugged helplessly. Some grinned sheepishly. Some tried to look as if it were perfectly normal to be standing on the tables, by casually slipping their hands into pockets, or studying the wall charts on musical notation and Beethoven. Those sitting down looked smug.

"Whose is this?" she asked.

"It's mine, Miss Dickenson," said Nathan. His voice seemed tiny in the now silent room.

"Good taste, Nathan," nodded Miss Dickenson.

Eyebrows shot up. Jaws went down. Sighs of relief hushed round the class. Some looked suspicious. It could be a trick.

"Like to do it again?" she asked.

"*Yes!*" they roared.

"I'm not deaf," laughed Miss Dickenson.

The tabletop chorus and orchestra grinned smugly as the seated ones put down their books and climbed awkwardly back onto the tables again.

"Thank you, Nathan," said Miss Dickenson, handing him the tape. "Not what I'd planned but it turned out to be a very interesting lesson."

110

"Yeah, thanks a lot, Nathe," said Steven as they turned into the corridor. "It was my turn on the synthesiser this week – I was looking forward to that. And I can't stand teachers who think they're trendy."

"Oh yeah – I didn't notice you complaining when you were up there with the rest of them, shouting your head off," said Nathan.

"That bit was all right," said Steven. "It was all that stuff after – the complete history of protest music and 'what's it trying to say' stuff."

"I think it was brilliant," butted in Nina. "Can I borrow it?"

"*We don't need no education!*" sang Steven, punching the air and stomping across the playground.

135.27, wrote Nathan.

Page thirteen calculator exercise finished.

There were nine of them in detention. He slid down in his chair, folded his arms and peered out of the window.

A nice sunny afternoon. The quest can begin at 16.30 hours. Need some dates and places first. No good asking Mum, though.

"Right, everybody. You may go now," said Miss Pickwick, looking up at the clock.

10
~
The Quest
~

"Now you're asking me something there, Nathan," said Nan. "Where did they meet? Let me think ... Was it on holiday? No, that was Julie – or was it Caroline? Trouble is, there were so many girls I lost track of them in the end."

"Dad?" said Nathan, wondering if Nan might be getting him mixed up with someone else.

"Oh yes. It was that group he was in, see. Had quite a following."

"Group?" said Nathan, wide-eyed, as if shock had left him unable to utter more than one word at a time.

"Hold on," said Nan. "There's a photo somewhere."

She rummaged in a drawer in the sideboard.

"Look, here's one of your grandad with his fishing-club trophy," said Nan.

"Yes, Nan."

"Oh, here's you on Father Christmas's knee at the Co-op – remember when I took you there, Nathan?"

"Yes, Nan."

"Now what's this? Yes – knew I had it somewhere."

Nathan took the photo. Five lanky, long-haired youths with flapping flares were performing on a small stage.

"Is that Dad with the headband and the furry waistcoat?"

"Probably," said Nan, peering over her glasses.

"I never knew Dad played the guitar."

"That was his first one, I think," said Nan. "He was still at school then – we bought it for his birthday. Of course he went all electronic later. Yes, look, there's Roger Harptree – they were in the same class. Harpo, they used to call him – runs the post office on the corner now."

"What, that big fat bald bloke with glasses?" said Nathan, staring down at the skinny boy with the mop of blond hair and heavy fringe.

"That's him," said Nan. "Now what did they use to call your dad? Buzz. That's it – Buzz. Oh, look – here's one of your mum. They'd just started going out then – can't forget that. It was the Christmas just before your grandad went into hospital – 1978. I remember him taking it – like it was yesterday. They were married three years later – pity your grandad wasn't there to see it."

Nathan stood up and peered down at it. A very young Mum with long straight hair squeezed between a young Dad in dark glasses and Nan, sitting on Nan's sofa.

"Was it famous – his group?"

"Don't think so, love. They used to travel about a bit though – pubs and clubs, colleges, things like that. *That's* where they met – I remember now – the Ten Bells. Your mum was working there when your dad's group played. Every Saturday night they used to do a turn. I wouldn't have paid to hear them. They used to practise in his room sometimes – when they couldn't find anywhere else. I just used to turn the radio up."

"What was it called – the group?"

"Purple something or other, I think," said Nan frowning.

"But they changed it several times. Tarantula – that was one of the names."

He ran all the way from Nan's to Bryjan. He delved into the front of his bag for the key.

Panting, he checked the time. He had a good twenty minutes before Dad got home. He unlocked the door and slipped in.

Using the loft pole, he released the loft door and lowered it till it dangled on its hinges. He pulled the ladder down with the hook, tested it and climbed up. Head and shoulders into the loft space, he switched on the light. He stared round him; cardboard boxes, suitcases, a roll of carpet, a lampshade and . . .

Yeah! I thought I was right! A guitar case!

He tugged the guitar from its dusty blue plastic cover.

It's the one in the photo – I'm sure it is.

He plucked the two remaining strings. They twanged mournfully.

I'll get it mended.

I've got dates.

I've got places.

I've got Dad's old guitar.

I've got Plan F.

And I've got the switch.

"Twenty-five pounds!" said Nathan.

"About that," nodded the man in the music shop, testing the neck of the guitar. "Needs some new tuning pegs, new strings, bridge needs some attention – a good old clean – but it's well worth doing. Cost you quite a bit to buy a new one like this."

"How long will it take?"

The man swivelled his mouth from side to side.

"Mm – got a lot on at the moment. Should be ready by Saturday, with a bit of luck."

"OK," said Nathan.

His pockets, bag, wallet and old chocolate-dispenser moneybox yielded eight pounds and thirty-one pence, a red tiddlywink, a hundred metre swimming medallion, a dead moth and a one franc coin. He raised some more by selling a computer game to Steven and his bicycle lock to Malcolm Hetherington.

But I'm still more than eight pounds short. Where am I going to get eight pounds by Saturday?

"I must be flavour of the week," said Nan when Nathan called on her after school on Tuesday. "Your mum popped in at lunch time. Doing well in her job, isn't she? Good luck to her, I say."

"Er – Nan ..."

"Just a sec, love. Let me finish this."

She sat down at the kitchen table, writing a shopping list on the back of an old envelope.

"Now – what else? All Bran, tinned peaches ..."

Nathan sipped his tea.

"Your windows could do with a clean, Nan."

"Where?" said Nan, looking up. "I only did them yesterday."

"What about your brasses, then. They could do with a polish."

"Wednesdays," said Nan, concentrating on her list. "I do the brasses Wednesdays. Before I go to Keep Fit."

"I could do them for you if you like," offered Nathan.

"Pr-ooo-ns," said Nan as she wrote it down, "and custard powder. Now have I forgotten anything?"

"Or dusting," said Nathan. "And I can wire plugs up. You don't need any plugs wiring up, do you, Nan?"

He got up and examined the plug on the kettle lead.

Nan fetched her shopping bag from the hook on the door and slipped her list into her handbag.

"Ah – so it's money you're after, is it, Nathan?" she said, peering hard at him, as if he had *I need some money* tattooed on his forehead.

Nathan gave what he thought might be a hopeful, but grateful, and at the same time, slightly apologetic smile. It wasn't easy.

"You'll get stuck like that if the wind changes," said Nan.

"It's not for me, Nan. It's for Dad. You'll never guess what I found in the loft – Dad's old guitar! The one in the photo. Well – I'm having it mended. It'll cost quite a lot – and I'm a bit short. I thought it would cheer him up like. What d'you think, Nan?"

"We-ell," said Nan, shaking her head, then, "yes," she interrupted herself, "I think it's a lovely idea, Nathan. A really lovely idea. Come along then, you can help me with the shopping."

"I can't read this at all, Nathan," said Nan. "I've brought the wrong glasses. What's that word say?"

Nathan squinted at it.

"It looks like gorilla."

"It can't be gorilla," said Nan. "Let me have another look – oh yes – it does look like gorilla."

"Excuse me," she said to a complete stranger leaning over the frozen chips, "can you make out what this says?"

"Garlic?" offered the man.

"What would I be wanting with garlic?" said Nan.

"Gherkins," said a lady, dithering over the biscuits. Nan shook her head.

"Looks like gerbil to me," said her little boy.

"No, it's definitely not gerbil," said Nan.

They were halfway home, having abandoned the "g" item, when Nan suddenly cried, "Gingernuts! That's what it was! I can't go without my gingernuts. Run back, Nathan, there's a love."

When he got back, Nan said, "You can do my brasses tomorrow, Nathan. If I'm not back from my Keep Fit, call at Mr Goldstein's next door. He's got the spare key. I better show you what to do first. I want it done properly, mind."

"Now," said Mr Onslow. "I've cast an eye over your 'Day in the Life of a Saxon' efforts. I've made comments in the margins – *read* them. Some have made a reasonable start,

117

but you need more historical detail – and *empathy*. Remember we talked about empathy? What's empathy? Yes, Malcolm."

"Putting yourself in someone else's place, Mr Onslow. Trying to understand what it felt like to be them."

Mr Onslow nodded.

"Sadly lacking here, I'm afraid," he said, picking one from the pile and putting on his glasses.

"Look – it's only two pages," muttered Nathan.

"*Only* two?" muttered Gav back. "I only managed one side."

"Now, although it may be absolutely fascinating to learn exactly what you were wearing – with detailed descriptions of your earrings, cloak, shoes, et cetera et cetera, as the Normans looted your home and killed your servants – and indeed it may have been very disconcerting to have your best brooch snatched from your cloak – but I think the slaughter of your servants and the slitting of your husband's throat before your eyes might have merited more than a single sentence. Some feeling of regret – danger – anguish – perhaps?" He tossed it onto the table.

"Ah, yes," he said, picking up another. "Some very imaginative variations on the spelling of the word *massacre*. Can we get that one sorted out, please? May I suggest the use of a dictionary? Yes, Steven?"

"How can you look it up in a dictionary if you don't know how to spell it, Mr Onslow?" He grinned to the class, as if expecting a round of applause for his cleverness.

"Oh – not that old chestnut again," sighed Mr Onslow.

"Well, I'll be happy to show you. Stay behind at break, Steven. Anyone else need a lesson on how to use a dictionary? No? Good. And may I add, Steven," he said, reaching to the top of the pile, "how very reassuring it is to have you in the class. To know that should we be suddenly invaded by the Norman advance, you – single-handed – will destroy the whole force. I'm sure King Harold would have welcomed you with open arms. The entire course of history would have been changed."

Steven shrugged modestly.

"But – sadly inaccurate – so some rewriting there, Steven."

One by one the homeworks were returned. At last Nathan saw Mr Onslow pick out his own effort. He recognised the green explosions.

"Ye gods!" muttered Gav. "Is that yours? You must have done huge writing."

"I'm not going to read this . . ." said Mr Onslow.

Because it's crap, groaned Nathan's head. *I've mucked it up. No good knowing stuff if you can't write it down properly.*

". . . because I want to ask the author to read it," finished Mr Onslow. "When I first read this – with some difficulty I may add – I suspected it might have been copied out from somewhere, so rich is it with insight and historical information, but on the evidence of the creative spelling and punctuation – where it exists – I'm convinced it must be all his own work. Come on, Nathan."

The author stumbled his way to the front. He saw Nickie say something behind her hand to Tansy. He saw Kevin

119

rolling his eyes. He saw Nina beaming at him. He saw Gav shaking his head in disbelief.

He felt himself grinning idiotically at the faces that stared expectantly up at him. He swallowed, shuffled his papers, took a breath and plunged in.

"I am Elfrida, daughter of Godwin ..."

Hoots of laughter prevented him from continuing. He felt the flush rise up his neck.

Great start, Nathe. You'll pay for this. It'll be the "Titian" catastrophe all over again. Why didn't you change Elfrida to a boy? 'Cos I didn't know I was going to have to read it out, did I?

"Carry on, Nathan," said Mr Onslow, when order had been restored.

"... I don't know where my father is – or my mother. The soldiers took them. I ran when they came – ran to my uncle's house. Now I live with him. But nowhere is safe. They take whatever they want. They make their own rules. I am too frightened to go out. People disappear all the time. Their punishments are swift and terrible. Days ago, a Norman was found with his throat slashed. They took a cruel revenge. Twenty people they rounded up at the marketplace. Men and women and children and babies. All put to the sword. Next time, they promised, it would be forty Saxon lives for one Norman. Then yesterday they came and took us. Smashed doors when people weren't fast enough in opening up, dragged whole families out. Everyone who lived here was taken. The old, the sick, the crippled. None of us knew why as they marched us away. For most of the morning we stood and waited. We were not allowed to speak. A girl who was ill and sat down was licked around the town—"

Puzzled glances passed round the classroom.

"Sorry," said Nathan, "I think that should be kicked — and I think I should have put a full stop after . . ."

"I recognise the problem," said Mr Onslow. "Try again."

". . . a girl who was ill and sat down was kicked. Around the town there had been rumours of another Norman being killed. We knew what the punishment would be. Only this time, we would pay a bloodier price.

"But this time it was different. The one they call Earl Ralf appeared, surrounded by his attendants and soldiers. He stood there in his fine clothes, whined his ugly foreign words while another translated. 'Let us remind you of the Norman law,' he told us. 'The forests and the woods belong to the king. Your king now. King William. Any man who trespasses on the king's property and takes what is not his is stealing from the king. Any man found trespassing with a bow in his hand is guilty. He will be punished. He will have his eyes put out. This is the law. You have eyes. Use them now. Watch and remember.'

"The soldiers dragged someone forward. He wasn't a man. Just a boy — thin, dirty, hungry-looking. I did not look as they did it. I tried not to hear, closed my ears, filled them with other sounds — my mother singing, my father laughing. I stared up at that ugly tower that crouches over us, watching — and I let the hate and anger burn into me. And after, when I looked at that poor boy — and the silent faces of those others who had been made to stand and watch

– I saw that hate burn in their eyes too. And I tell you this, if hate were fire, then not one Norman would live. They would burn. Here first. And then in hell.

"There are worse things. Alfred – my cousin, my uncle's son – came home with terrible news. I pray that he is wrong – but ..."

"I think we'll stop there, Nathan. Well done," said Mr Onslow.

There were choruses of "Go on!" and disappointed "Ohs".

"Just as it was getting interesting," complained Steven.

"It's also very long," said Mr Onslow, "and would take up more time than we have to spare at the moment. I'm sure, however, it has put you in the mood and eager to get back to your own work. Thank you, Nathan. One of the best pieces of work I've had in some time."

"That reference to William's visit to the castle – where did you get that from?" asked Mr Onslow quietly, bending over Nathan's desk.

"I sort of – well – saw it in my head."

"You imagined it? Fine. Highly unlikely that he ever visited the castle of course. But an interesting thought. Now why don't you set this up on the word processor and see to your corrections?"

" 'Ere, look, it's Elfrida, innit?" shouted Neil as Nathan and Gav entered the changing rooms.

"What you doin' in 'ere?" said Kevin, barring his way. "This is the boys' changing rooms."

Sniggers.

He was trying to think of a clever but deadly response when someone grabbed him round his neck from behind. Hands yanked at his legs. His feet slid from under him. Then he was being dragged across the floor to the door.

"Yeah – you oughta be with the other girls, with your new sister – Tansy," sneered Ricky.

"What? Get off!" he yelled, kicking.

But the hands grasping his trousers just gripped tighter. He saw Neil, Kevin, and Ricky grinning down at him.

Suddenly, Gav was there, and Steven, and Tim, all brandishing rulers like swords.

"Let go, you Norman pigs!" yelled Steven, cutting the air with his ruler and lunging with a sudden thrust.

They sliced and parried, dancing to and fro like boxers. Then Tim whirled his ruler round his head like a double-handed sword and gave a wild cry. The air whistled over their heads as other Saxon supporters in various states of undress urged them on. The Norman pigs ducked, dropped Nathan and fled. A cheer went up.

Nathan lay spreadeagled on his back, his blazer half off where they'd dragged him by the sleeves.

What do they mean – my new sister – what's going on?

"You OK, Nathe?" said Gav, leaning over.

"Yes, thank you, my faithful servants."

He sat up and reached for his shoe which had come off.

"As a reward you can have half my kingdom and – if you're really lucky – my hand in marriage."

"Ugh! No, thanks," grimaced Gav, wiping his hands on his trousers.

"What are you doing down there, Beazer?" said Mr Cosby.

"Hey, Nathe, wait for me!" cried Gav as Nathan hoisted his bag and headed for the door.

"Can't — gotta see my nan," shouted Nathan, trotting backwards.

He ran across the playground.

Do Nan's brasses and, with a bit of luck, time for a quick switchback — if I get there early.

"Hi! Nathe!"

It was Nina, sitting on the wall by the gates. She stood up and walked towards him.

"Thanks for the loan," she said, holding out the tape.

"S'ok." He nodded and carried on walking.

She trotted alongside him.

"You at your dad's still?"

"My nan's — gotta hurry — she's expecting me."

"I liked the guitar bits. I play the guitar — well, learning — nearly a year now."

"Yeah?" shrugged Nathan, increasing his pace.

"After school, on Fridays, with Miss Dickenson. And sometimes we get together at lunch times. It's beginning to sound OK."

"I've got to go this way," said Nathan, turning into an alleyway.

"Is it true your mum's going out with Tansy's dad, then?" she asked.

Nathan slowed and stopped. "What's all this Tansy stuff about?"

"Well, her dad and your mum – you know – everyone's seen them – together like. I saw them in a car."

"He's giving her driving lessons, that's all."

"It's just that Tansy says—"

"What? What'd she say?"

"Well – it's more what the others are saying really."

"What others? What are they saying?"

"Oh – you know – Kevin, Neil – that lot – they keep saying—"

"What? What?"

"Look – perhaps I shouldn't have said – you know what they're like. Best to ignore it really. Perhaps I shouldn't have said – look, I've got to go – sorry."

She ran off.

11

~

Without You, None of This
Would Have Happened

~

Thanks a lot, Nina.

Nathan let himself in with the key Mr Goldstein had
given him.

Calm down, Nathe. Concentrate. Think about Plan F.
Nan might turn up any minute – don't waste time thinking
about those nerdheads. Everything depends on this. You
gotta get it right. Anyway, in the very near future Smelly
Mike is going to be ancient history.

Nan had left everything ready for him on the newspaper-
covered kitchen table. She'd shown him what to do. He
shook the can, spread the white cream onto the cloth and
smeared it on the fire tongs, the shovel, the big bowl and
the plate, the toasting fork with the Witch of Wookey
handle, and the two kneeling pixies, then left them to dry
while he fetched his switch.

He ran upstairs to the room which had once been Dad's.
There was a bed, an old-fashioned wardrobe with two
drawers and a long mirror. Nan's sewing machine stood on a
table beneath the window and pieces of material pinned to
paper shapes were spread out on the bed.

What did Nan say? 1978. And if this is where they
sometimes practised, should be able to find something.

His hands were sweating. He wiped them on his shirt, fiddled with the dials, switched on and pressed the button.

Just the hum. Not connecting. Try again. No. What about over there? Still no luck. Try 1979 – over there. No. Keep trying. Here we go!

It hummed and locked. The lights flickered and faded.

Funny. The hum's still going. Oh, great. I'm Nan. 1979 version, trundling round Dad's room with a vacuum cleaner. I can do better things with my time, thanks. But hold on – let's take a look around. What a difference. Can't see the walls for posters and stuff. Stacks of records, clothes, piles of stuff – on the chair and over the floor. There's his guitar. Not the one in the photo – that's hanging on the wall. No this one's white, electric, slim. Oops – hang about – me and Nan are changing nozzles, clicking on a brush thingy – off we go again – we're dusting down his guitar for him – now along the skirting board – changing back nozzles and – under the bed we go. Making a spluttering noise – what's this flapping from the nozzle? Your pants, Dad. Bending down – under the bed now – a fair old number of socks here – and Nan's having a right old grumble. This is boring.

He took his finger off the button, readjusted the dials and tried again. And again. And more agains.

Come on! Come on! Nan'll be home soon.

He perched on the bed, reset the dials, and pressed.

At last! Here we go – I'm switching. Who am I? It's a bit crowded in here. I'm not Mum – she's over there, sitting on the floor. There's Dad – and Harpo – and another.

They're fiddling with their guitars, twanging away. What a row!

He released the button, crossed the room to the spot where he'd seen Mum sitting, and reswitched.

Yeah! I'm Mum. It's all happening. I'm staring up at Dad. He's not taking much notice though – yet I know he knows I'm watching. He's showing off a bit now, sliding his fingers up and down the strings, making them sing. I'm staring up and I've got this great soppy-gooey feeling and I'm thinking, What nice hands he's got – and what lovely eyes. He winks at me and – *Just remember, Nathe, it's Mum, not you* – yeah, Mum's thinking, Oh, he's so dreamy, he's so – so . . .

This is embarrassing – I can't take this – quick – switch off.

Nathan shook himself.

Weird. Really weird. Feel like a melted Mars Bar. I can't go through that again. It's not normal, is it? I don't want to end up falling in love with my 1979 dad. But I was right, wasn't I?

Yeah! I was *right*!

He leapt to his feet. Ran round the room, cheering himself with a roaring crowd noise at the back of his throat. This was scoring the winning goal in the World Cup. He pounded his chest and cried, *"Yes!"*

You had it once, Dad. And I've found it! Your charisma. All we've got to do now is put it back. If we can make Mum feel about you like she did then, it can't fail. Smelly Mike's going to be exterminated. Nathan the Exterminator.

By the time Nan got back, the kitchen table gleamed with polished brass.

He stopped outside Mum's. A silver XR3 was parked on the double yellow lines. He looked around hopefully for a traffic warden.

He let himself in. Mike was leaning against the fridge, wiring a plug to a lamp. Mum was standing by the cooker, laughing. Look at him! Who's he think he is? That's not his job. What you doing, Mum? You're letting him take over!

He waited for Mum to notice him, dropped his bag and, turning his back to her, went into his room and shut the door.

"You're not going to be silly, are you, Nathan?" said Mum, following him in.

Arms folded, she stood looking down at him where he lay on the bed counting the number of dead flies trapped in the light fitting. She sat on the edge of the bed. He rolled over, went to the window, opened it and leant out. He could see Mike's car below. He saw him emerge from the building. He had an enormous urge to leap out and jump on him. He watched him unlock the car door and slide in.

Mum was standing behind him now. She put her hand on his shoulder.

"Get off!"

He wriggled away.

"You lied," he said, throwing himself across the bed. "You said 'truce'."

"I meant it. But I didn't say I'd let you blackmail me into how I run my life."

He put the pillow over his head.

"Now you just listen to me," she said, snatching it from him. "Fact one: I need to learn to drive. Fact two: I can't afford to pay for lessons. Fact three: I am going to continue having lessons from Mike. Fact four: I am now going for a lesson. Fact five: I shall be having a lesson every day, so you'd better get used to it. Got all that? If you want to behave like a spoiled baby, then carry on. It just makes life a little more difficult, that's all. But I am not going to have you telling me what I can and can't do. I've had enough of that. Now I'm going – your dinner's in the oven."

He felt the mattress bounce as she stood up.

"I'll see you later. Driving lessons. That's all it is, Nathan. Nothing more. Just driving lessons."

She walked to the door.

"It's not just driving lessons! It's wiring plugs as well! I'm the person who wires plugs round here. You didn't ask me, did you? Oh, yeah – and how come everyone's saying you're going out with him, then?" yelled Nathan.

"Who's everyone?"

"Kids, kids at school, they've seen you together."

"I'm not surprised. We drive round the estate regularly for practice. Well – you'd just better put them straight, hadn't you, Nathan?"

So when Kevin asked him if it was true that Tansy would soon be his sister and was he going to change his name to

Nathan Nott - or perhaps Elfrida Nott — and was he going to be a bridesmaid and how his mum must be really hard up if Tansy's dad was the best she could do, et cetera, et cetera, Nathan took the opportunity to demonstrate a wrestling tackle he'd once seen Big Daddy perform on television. Afterwards Gav said it was probably the element of surprise that made it seem so easy, rather than expertise, plus the fact that Tansy and Nina were sitting on his legs while he, Steven and Tim helped by preventing Neil and Ricky from joining in. And Kevin apologised very nicely.

"And we've got witnesses, right?" said Gav, nodding his head to the crowd that had gathered. A small cheer went up.

"Thanks, Nathe," said Nina later. "He's been a total pain. Him and his loonies have been having a go at Tansy. She's been really upset."

"Yeah, thanks, Nathe — and Gav," said Tansy.

"The least I could do," they said.

Each day, after school, he went to Nan's. He'd shopped, he'd polished, he'd vacuum-cleaned. Nan was there most of the time. Then, on Thursday, as he was cleaning the oven, she called, "Just popping round the corner to see my friend Beatty. Won't be long."

He dashed upstairs. It was five minutes before he managed a switch.

Yeah — this is it. Here we go.

I'm Dad! Standing in front of the mirror — posing with my white guitar — music blasting out. But it's not coming from me – not even plugged in. Must be a record or a tape . . .

"*I don't like Mondays*," it sings – and I'm singing along – watching myself in the mirror – looking really mean and moody. I stop and examine myself from one side – then from the other. Doing the old silent fingerwork now, holding the guitar up and then down. Really skinny, a right beanpole. And look at that hair, Dad. I mean – sideburns! Tight jeans, boots, scruffy shirt. Stopping now, reaching for the dark glasses. Off we go again. What we doing? Walking over to – a record player – switching off – lowering the arm in the first groove – plugging in the guitar – back to the mirror again – trying out the strings – trying to copy—

"Nathan? Where are you?"

He froze, strode with giant careful steps to the door, and tiptoed into the bathroom. He flushed the lavatory, loosened his shirt, pulled it over the switch and, whistling loudly, opened the door and ran downstairs.

"Oh! You're back! Didn't hear you . . ."

"You haven't got very far with the oven," said Nan.

"Burnt in stains, Nan," said Nathan. "Difficult to shift. Left it to soak for a bit."

"Here you are then, Nathan," said Nan on Saturday morning after he'd helped her with the shopping. She held out two five pound notes.

"I hope it's enough – it's all I can manage, love. Can't do this on a regular basis though."

"Aw, thanks, Nan. That's great. Got enough now."

He gave her a peck on the cheek.

"And the best of luck," she called.

As he hurried towards Dad's with the guitar case, he saw his reflection in Dixons' window.

Wipe that stupid smirk off your face, Nathe.

But he couldn't help himself.

"My old guitar, Nathe! I can't believe it! Where'd you find it? This is amazing! Why – it's perfect. Did you do this, Nathe? Well, well – forgotten all about this."

Dad tugged it from the case.

"Let's tune it in, eh."

He strummed a rippling chord.

"Still sounds good – fingers a bit rusty though – just need a bit of practice . . ."

He performed several rapid chord changes. His fingers plucked and the notes danced.

"Great stuff, Dad."

Mum's suitcases stood in the hall, waiting to be unpacked.

A streamlined Dad in jeans and a white T-shirt strummed his guitar. Mum gazed up at him from the sofa.

"I'm sorry, Bryan. It was all a big mistake. You know me – act first, think later. But I'm back now – now and for ever – thanks to Nathe."

Dad stopped strumming.

"Yeah – thanks, kid. It's all down to you. Without you

none of this would have happened. Gee, we're lucky parents!"

A screech of brakes! A honking horn. Something large and red coming towards him – falling. The slam of a car door.

"You stupid kid! You crazy or something – walking out like that! Why don't you watch where you're going?"

Legs – surrounded by legs. A face . . .

"Are you all right? Can you stand? Does it hurt anywhere?"

"Perhaps someone ought to call an ambulance?"

Nathan sat in the middle of the road clutching the guitar.

"No, I'm OK. Sorry, sorry."

He stumbled off.

"Come in here, love. You better sit down for a minute – just to be sure."

It was a lady in the Fresh 'n' Fruity Greengrocery.

"Come into the shop for a bit."

She sat him down on a chair at the back.

"What about the guitar – what about the guitar?" said Nathan.

"Well, let's have a look, shall we? Where d'you live, son? Perhaps we ought to get in touch with your mum and dad."

"No – it's OK. I'm OK."

"Looks all right to me," said the lady, unzipping the case. "How many strings should it have?"

"Six."

"All present and correct."

She handed it back to him. He checked it over. It seemed OK.

"Now, are you sure you're all right?"

He stood up. His legs and arms still worked. Just a bit shaky, that's all.

"Great, thanks."

"Is there anything else we can do? Ring your mum perhaps?"

"Just one thing," said Nathan, checking the loose change in his pocket.

"What, love?"

"Could I have a pound of tomatoes, a lettuce and a cucumber, please?"

12
~
Play It Dad, Play It
~

"This is it, is it?" said Dad, looking down at the lettuce leaf, four slices of cucumber and the tomato on his plate. He lifted the lettuce with his knife and peered under it as if hoping to find something more substantial beneath.

"My treat," said Nathan. "You don't have to pay me or anything."

The guitar was hidden in the cupboard under the stairs where he'd sneaked it in. He was saving it up.

"Isn't there anything to go with it?" said Dad.

"There's loads more," said Nathan, nodding towards the brown bags on the draining board.

"Well, I'm not going to get fat on this, am I?" said Dad, spearing a slice of cucumber with his fork.

"You're getting into some very unhealthy eating habits, Dad," accused Nathan with his fork. "We've been doing it in Food Technology."

"Food *what*?"

"Did you know you could be dead by fifty if you carry on like you are."

"Thank you, Nathan. That's cheered me up enormously."

"I mean it, Dad. For instance, did you know that one in three men suffer from heart disease – caused by high-risk factors like unbalanced diet, fatty foods, lack of exercise, overweight? You see, what happens is you get a build-up of fatty deposits in the arteries ..."

With his fork, he drew huge football-sized fatty deposits in front of Dad's chest.

"... they get totally bunged up – blood can't get to the heart – then suddenly – bang!"

Dad jumped slightly.

"Before you know it – you're a goner."

"Can we talk about something else, Nathan?"

Congratulations, Nathe. Much more tactful than telling him he's an oversized couch potato. Now eat up your lettuce. Yuk. I hate lettuce. This had better be worth it.

"What about this Mike business?" said Dad. "Has he been around lately?"

"Afters," said Nathan, setting a small apple before Dad. This had been an additional purchase when he'd discovered he had enough money for a pound of apples.

"I've got some doughnuts in the cupboard," said Dad.

"Fatty deposits, Dad. Now wait there. And don't move."

He ran to the hall cupboard and took out the guitar. His hands trembled and his chest throbbed. He felt like an astronaut waiting to be launched.

Except they wouldn't feel as nervous as I'm feeling right now.

Dad had his back to him, elbows on the table, munching his apple.

"Don't turn round yet."

He stood behind Dad's chair and held the guitar in front of him like a cello.

137

"Right – you can look – *now*."

Dad turned, looked, took another bite from his apple.

"Don't you recognise it, Dad?"

Dad chewed thoughtfully.

"It's yours, Dad. Look!"

Nathan handed it to him.

"Go on! Look – look inside."

Dad balanced his core on the table, unzipped the case and unpeeled it like a banana skin.

"So it is. Well, well – you've been poking around in the loft, eh? What are you going to do with it, then?"

"It's all been cleaned up – new strings, everything," said Nathan, rushing forward, unable to restrain himself any longer. "There's even a new plectrum, that's for plucking the strings."

"I know what a plectrum is, Nathan," said Dad.

"Go on, Dad, have a go."

"You can't just have a go, Nathan. It'll need tuning."

"Go on then, Dad. Tune it."

"Not now, Nathan, eh?"

"Go on, Dad. Please."

Dad sighed, held down a string, listened, turned the tuning peg, plucked and listened, held another, played them together, twanging and listening his way through each string. Then he positioned his fingers on the fret and ran the plectrum over the strings. They sang harmoniously. He strummed a few chords, gave it a pat – and handed it back.

"There you go then."

138

"It's not for me, Dad – it's for you."

"Don't be daft, Nathan. What am I going to do with it?"

"Play it, Dad. Like you used to. Nan said – she said you used to be in a group."

"Oh, your nan . . . She put you up to this has she?"

"No, Dad. Aw – come on, Dad. You used to sound good—"

"How could you possibly know that, Nathan?"

"I just know!" he cried, fists clenched with impatience and frustration.

"Well, you're wrong there, Nathan. The truth is I wasn't good enough – and not-good-enough isn't good enough for me," said Dad, leaning the guitar against the chair.

"I don't mind, Dad. What you did just now – that sounded good – to me. Just do it for me, Dad."

"You grew out of playing with Lego, remember, Nathan," said Dad, standing and hitching up his trousers. "Well, I grew out of playing the guitar. Now just leave it, will you?"

Nathan watched him stack the plates and take them over to the sink.

This isn't what was meant to happen – he's spoiling everything! It was meant to be fireworks – rockets and bangers – not a dud sparkler. He should be leaping around the room – strutting and strumming! He's just so – so pathetic!

"Go on, Dad! Please!"

"I told you, Nathan. Leave it."

139

"Well, if – if you won't do it for me, do it for Mum. She liked it – I know she did."

"You know nothing, Nathan," said Dad, not even turning round.

"How do you know what I know!" shouted Nathan. "You'd be surprised by what I know! And I know one thing" – he was almost crying now – "you're pathetic! You know that? Really pathetic!"

Now Dad turned.

"And where did you get that from – your mother? You sound just like her – you know that?"

"Oh yeah!" yelled Nathan. "Well, that's funny – 'cos she says I'm like you. Funny how I end up with all the horrible bits of both of you, isn't it! And I'll tell you something else – she's not coming back—"

"When I want your opinion, I'll ask for it, thank you," interrupted Dad, wiping his hands on the tea towel. "Now I want to catch the news."

"You're not listening, Dad!"

Nathan could feel the moisture building up behind his eyes.

"Oh, I can hear you, Nathan. They can probably hear you on the other side of the by-pass."

He walked out of the kitchen.

"Listen, Dad! Please!"

He stood watching him disappear into the sitting room. He heard the television click on. Anger and disappointment swelled inside him and rushed up in a tidal wave. He ran after him.

"She's not coming back!" he yelled. "That's right! Turn the volume up. Talking to you is like – like talking to a – a brick wall! A bloomin' brick wall! That's what you are! Well – I'm telling you – she's never coming back. And do you know something? I don't blame her! 'Cos you're a real pain! You feel so sorry for yourself, don't you! Well, I don't care – 'cos I'm not coming back either! Do you hear?" he screamed. "Do you hear!"

He rushed out, through the back door and across the road. Chest heaving, he slowed into a walk. He walked and walked. One street blurred into another. *She's never coming back.* And he knew that he'd known that for a long time. Mum was never going back. He couldn't make it happen. Not even with the switch. He couldn't change the past. He could only look at it.

He sat in the dusk of Abbeyfield Gardens.

Stupid. Nathan the Stupid. Just kidding yourself, Nathe. Who do you think you are? Stupid switch. Stupid. Stupid. Stupid. Everyone's stupid.

Mum was out when Nathan got up late on Sunday. Her note said she'd gone for driving practice. He slumped before the bathroom mirror over the basin.

Nathan the Slitty-eyed Shock-haired Zombie. Plan F down the— Shut up – shut up. Stupid plans.

"Aren't you dressed yet, Nathe?" said Mum, bursting in and disturbing his gloom.

She waited for a response from the body face down on the sofa, legs splayed, one arm dangling lifelessly, face twisted

141

towards the television screen where an animated duck in a Red Indian headdress was being pursued by a lasso-twirling wolf in a cowboy hat.

"It's a lovely day. You ought to be out with your friends – not stuck in front of the telly."

Yeah, I'll pedal down to the rec on my trike, thought Nathan, and we can all play on the roundabout.

Mum started to sing as she filled the kettle. Her cheeriness intensified his irritation and anger.

"Want a coffee, Nathe?"

"Unngg."

"I'll take that as a *yes*, shall I?"

She put it on a tray below his dangling hand.

"Move over, then," she said, almost sitting on him.

Go away! he wanted to shout. *Leave me alone!*

"Are you really watching this, Nathe?"

"Unngg!"

"I'll turn it off, then."

He saw a strange woman lean forward. This wasn't his mother. His mother had long hair, bushy, with curly bits. This mother had cropped hair, like a boy's, sleeked back.

"What you done to your hair?"

"Don't you like it?"

"Saw-rye," he mumbled.

He dragged his legs from where they were trapped behind Mum's back, leaned his head on his knees and stared at his big toe.

"I want to talk to you, Nathe. It's something important. Look – I can't talk to the top of your head."

She fiddled with the handle of her coffee mug.

"I was called to see the manager a few days ago. He had a visitor – one of the sales directors from Brindles' head office in London – but it was me he really wanted to see. I didn't tell you straight away – needed to think things through."

Nathan yawned.

Mum carried on. The words washed over him like a lullaby: creative sales, innovative ideas, market trends . . . he was in the Saxon marketplace again. *Fish, fresh fish!*

"Have you understood what I'm saying, Nathan?"

"What?"

"They're offering me a new job – as a buyer! They want to expand my ideas on hand-made and crafted pots! Can you believe it? They want me to find new suppliers, set up a small sales department here at Brindles and later, if it works, to introduce the idea to other stores around the country. It'll be on a trial basis at first – and I'll have to go on a training course – but it means – listen to this, Nathe – a company car! And a proper salary and . . ."

Nathan slid down the sofa.

Big deal. Now leave me alone. I want to sleep.

"You don't mind, then?" said Mum.

He shrugged.

"You understand what it means?"

Was this a trick question?

"Well, as it appears to make no difference to you, I'll tell them yes, then, shall I? I thought you might have shown a bit more interest, though, Nathan. I don't think you realise how unusual this is — what it means to me. It's quite an achievement, you know."

She stood up. She hadn't drunk any of her coffee.

"You'd better talk to your dad, then, seeing as he doesn't like my hotchpotch arrangements — warn him."

"Warn him? Why? What's it got to do with him?" asked Nathan.

"Well, you've got to go somewhere when I'm away, Nathan."

She looked down at him.

"You haven't been listening, have you, Nathan?" she sighed.

She leaned down.

"If I'm going to take this job, which — as you don't seem to care one way or other — I shall, it'll mean, Nathan, that I'll be away at least three days a week. That's what I've been trying to tell you. Got it? It's you I'm thinking of, Nathan. When I'm away, you'll have to stay with your Dad, OK?"

It's you that I'm thinking of, Nathan. Isn't that what Dad said?

"Do what you like." He shrugged.

He levered himself up and slouched back to bed.

"Nathe? Are you all right?"

"I'll stay with Nan," he said, shutting the door behind him.

13
~
I Don't Like Mondays
~

Question 1. How much water will be displaced by a brick measuring . . .

Nathan looked around. All heads were down. He stared out of the classroom window where tiny distant figures were running round the sports field.

He'd dreamed about bricks. Lego bricks: red, yellow, blue, black and white. He had been trying to build something with them. Couldn't remember what. He'd been made of Lego himself. A little Lego boy with a stiff plastic cap of orange hair. The bricks wouldn't fit together properly – he'd got angry – kicked them down with his little black Lego foot.

He could feel the anger now. In his head, his shoulders, his chest, the fist holding his pen. And he was shouting at Dad again, looking down at him in his armchair.

Yeah, he even had a doughnut in his hand, didn't he? *After all the trouble I went to and all . . .*

And suddenly there was Mum, walking down the path with her suitcases to the waiting taxi, not even a glance backwards. Now he was back in the kitchen and a great plunging ache filled his insides. *Don't be daft, Nathan. You know nothing, Nathan.*

"Nathan! No wonder you know nothing. You won't find the answers out of the window, lad."

Nathan looked up at Mr Yates's face.

Hey – teacher – leave us kids alone, he wanted to shout.

"Well – thank you for joining us at last," said Mr Yates.

There were a few titters.

"We're looking at question seven. Perhaps you'd like to come and show us how *you* did it."

He held out a piece of chalk as an invitation to the blackboard.

"I haven't got to number seven yet."

"Well – what a surprise. You're a complete time-waster, aren't you, Nathan Beazer? I don't know why you bother coming to lessons at all. I've just had about enough of—"

The anger bubbled inside Nathan. He was a shaken cola can – he was fizzing inside – he was going to explode – any second – now! He shot up from his seat. His chair clattered to the floor. Thirty heads pivoted. Mr Yates's jaw clenched.

"I don't care!" yelled Nathan.

"Clare – give these out," said Mr Yates, grabbing a pile of worksheets, "and you, Nathan, come with me. You're going straight to—"

Nathan picked up his maths textbook and tossed it through the open window.

"That's how much I care!" he yelled.

He ran out to the front. Mr Yates tried to make a grab. Nathan dodged sideways.

"Just calm down now, Nathan," said Mr Yates, trying a different tactic and holding out an arm like a peace offering.

Nathan grabbed the pile of papers from Clare, who stood

mesmerised by the scene, and tossed them upwards. They hit the strip lighting and drifted down as if in slow motion. He darted for the door and ran out into the corridor, dragged the DON'T RUN notice from the pinboard, tore it in two and threw it at Mr Yates who was coming out of the door. He charged on, one outstretched arm scattering a carefully arranged display of books.

"Get away from the door at once – back to your seats – now!" he heard Mr Yates ordering.

A group of four composing a poem on a word processor found themselves staring at a blank screen as Nathan raged past, pausing just long enough to pull the plug from its socket. Shouts of "Oy – get off!" and "Look out!" and "What did he do that for?" reverberated behind him.

A small girl delivering a message saw the note snatched from her hand, crumpled and tossed out of a window. He stormed on, propelled by something he couldn't control, sweeping all before him, leaving a trail of debris in his wake: spilled books, overturned tables and chairs. Behind him, dazed students set to picking things up, including themselves, from the floor.

On he rampaged till finally, in the entrance hall, by the front door, he came to a halt. A carefully arranged display of clay heads stared at him, almost daring him to strike – and suddenly he was empty. Drained. A hand fell on to his shoulder.

"I think you'd better come with me, don't you?"

Mrs Sanderson, deputy head, steered him towards her office.

Dear Sally,
   I am sorry I took your library book and stuffed
it down the radiater.
      Nathan Beazer

Six down, thirteen to go.

Nathan sat in Mrs Sanderson's office writing letters of apology.

Mrs Sanderson put down her phone.

"Apparently your father's out on a delivery and your mother's in London. Is there anyone else I can contact, Nathan?"

"There's my nan."

Dear Clive,
   I am sorry that I tore your pict—

"Excuse me – I'm Mrs Beazer – Nathan's grandmother . . ."

The out-of-breath voice came from the secretary's office beyond the door.

Nathan stood before Mrs Sanderson, who was seated at her desk. She had just given an account of Nathan's behaviour in the maths lesson. Nan sat on a chair to the left of him, looking down at her handbag.

"Now, Nathan, I'm going to describe to your grand-mother exactly what you did in the corridor – I saw it all very clearly from the top where I happened to be coming out of a classroom. If you think I'm being inaccurate or unfair, you must say so when I've finished."

Nathan nodded and glanced at Nan. She looked worried but gave him a micro smile.

Mrs Sanderson began her tale. Nathan listened with rapt attention as it unfolded.

Did I do all that?

"... then finally, in the entrance hall, you threw a potted plant at the staff photos before coming to a stop, thankfully, before Year Eleven's GCSE art work display."

Nan was looking down at her handbag again, shaking her head.

"Have I described that accurately, Nathan?" asked Mrs Sanderson, leaning back in her chair. "Is that what you did?"

Nan looked up hopefully.

Nathan stared at the stapler on Mrs Sanderson's desk.

"I think I must have done – if you saw it," he said.

"Don't you remember, Nathan?"

"I remember tearing up the notice."

Mrs Sanderson leaned forward, clasping her hands together on the desk before her.

"Well – what do you have to say, Nathan?" she said.

Nan swivelled in her chair to look at him. His mind searched desperately for the right words. Nan gave him an encouraging nod. They waited. All at once the words came to him, something Nan had once said. Something she'd told him to remember. He straightened his shoulders and stared straight ahead.

"No one's perfect, Mrs Sanderson."

Mrs Sanderson closed and opened her eyes very slowly, lowered her head and covered her face with one hand, as if deep in thought. Nan looked crumpled.

"All right, Nathan. I'll speak to you later, wait outside, will you? I'd like a chat with your grandmother first."

He was on report. For two weeks. Each lesson, the teacher would have to fill in his sheet regarding his conduct. He would have to spend all his break times in Mrs Sanderson's office and report to her at the end of each day with his sheet. Letters would be sent to his mother and father.

Sometimes, thought Mrs Sanderson as she filed Nathan's record cards away, we might achieve more if we could put a parent or two on report.

14
~
Looking Forward to the Past
~

"*Happy birthday, dear Nathan, happy birthday to you!*" he sang to himself along with all the others. He was in the kitchen at Dad's, switched back to his fifth birthday party.

I'm some kid called Martin – don't remember inviting him – but I'm definitely him, 'cos Mum's saying, "The iced gems are for eating, Martin, not for throwing." I can see I'm having a great time – chubby-faced little kid in my new T-shirt blowing out the candles on my football cake. Now it's present time. "Yippee!" I'm yelling. "A Postman Pat jigsaw puzzle and Jellytots! Thanks!"

Nathan switched off, smiling, and repositioned himself in the sitting room ready for watching pass-the-parcel.

I'm Gav now – oi, Sime, pass it on, the music's started. Yeah – I remember this bit. This is where I have to do a forfeit. Mum's reading it out: "Hop round the room like a frog." Everyone's killing themselves. Nan's gonna fall off her chair if she's not careful. Dad's taking a photo. "Croak croak," I'm going.

The game finished. Nathan switched off and stood there letting the laughter and happiness seep through him. It was intoxicating. He was King of the Castle, Lord of the Jungle, World Champion of everything. He felt he only had to flip his body and he'd fly into a triple back somersault. He checked behind him.

Nah – not enough room. Or time – heck, it's nearly a quarter to six – Dad'll be home soon.

He grabbed his things, slammed the door behind him, leapt the gate and headed back to the flat, hopscotching the cracks in the pavement, dashing across the road, causing a bike to swerve and brake suddenly. Running backwards he gave a cheery wave at the angry cyclist.

He visited Dad's every day after school now. Would slip in, set up his switch and search for the good times. Then he'd slip away before Dad got back. He couldn't face Dad. He wouldn't know what to say. Being on report wasn't so bad; quite useful in its way. It gave him an excuse to evade all questions and explanations. He'd been mobbed on his return to the classroom.

"What'd they say, Nathe?"

"You were amazing! What happened?"

"You should have seen old Yates's face."

And Gav asking, "What's got into you, Nathe? What's up?"

And Nina's, "You all right, Nathe? You went white, really white."

He didn't want to talk about it. Even to Mum. He let Nan tell her. He didn't know if Mum knew about the guitar or not. Nan had got it out of him, though, and had listened with a grim face. But Mum had been making a big fuss over him lately and asking questions. Too many questions.

Why go over all that again? I want to forget all that. I've got better things to do, haven't I? I've still got the switch.

Forget about history, forget about plans and quests. That was all stupid. I've found what the switch is for – chasing the good times. Not doing anyone any harm, am I?

He'd sit in class, willing the clock hands forward to when he could grab his bag and go, wishing the day away, looking forward to the past. He'd watched most of his birthdays now and a couple of Christmases. There was more to come and, right now, he didn't want anything else.

"What? What?" said Nathan, opening his eyes. "Where am I? Is this a switchback? What's that noise? Where's the switch? What's going on?"

Slowly, the room came into focus. He reached out a hand to turn off the alarm.

"What – nine o'clock? It can't be!"

He jumped out of bed. Hammering the alarm. But it wouldn't switch off. That was because it wasn't switched on. The ringing was coming from the phone.

He stumbled towards it.

Why didn't Mum wake me up?

"Yeah," he said to the phone.

"It's Gav."

"Who?"

"Gav! What's the matter with you – I've been ringing for ages. I thought you were dead or something."

"No – I'm not dead. Look – what is it? I'm late—"

"Late for what?"

"School. Here – where you ringing from?"

"Nathe – it's Saturday!"

"Oh – right," said Nathan, trying to unscramble his brains.

"Dad's taking us to Bournemouth again. He says you can come if you want – we've got this new extension thingy to sleep in – bring a snorkel if you—"

"Sorry, Gav – can't – sorry."

He put the phone back. It blurred, stretched, separated into two identical phones and then snapped back into one. He stared at it for a few seconds, rubbed his eyes and staggered back to his bed.

It's all your own fault, Nathe. You've done some pretty heavy switching lately. It's doing your brain in. But if you want the buzzes – gotta put up with the fuzzes. If you want the switches – gotta take the twitches.

The side effects had developed a pattern. Stage One, The Buzz, was the zooming of energy and exhilaration – like bingeing on happiness. Stage Two, The Yawns, brought the lethargy and exhaustion, dragging him into sleep. Stage Three was The Fuzzes, or Scrambled Brains; he was in Stage Three now. When reality and switches got mixed up. When he couldn't remember where he was or who he was. When he'd wake up at night not sure if he was asleep or awake – or in a switch. Stage Four, The Twitches, followed rapidly. The Fidgets, Mum called them. Even she had noticed. She'd looked at him suspiciously, peered into his eyes, mentioned the doctor. "And I'm not joking this time, Nathe."

Even now his fingers were drumming.

"Oh no!"

He sat up.

If it's Saturday, I can't go to Dad's, can I? He'll be there. I can't switch!

Mild panic washed over him.

Calm down — it's no big deal. There's got to be some other place.

Then he remembered Nick's old shed.

Yeah — loads of good times there.

Shed's still here.

He could just see its roof over the fence. Someone else lived here now. The back gate in the fence was locked, but through a knothole he could see a small, neat garden and a child's swing.

Used to be a right dump when Nick lived here — good laugh though.

The garden backed on to the recreation ground, screened by clumps of bushes. Where the fence stood had once been a dipping stretch of wire netting.

There used to be a hole in it. That's how we used to get in — anything to avoid coming face to face with Nick's brother.

He stood roughly where he remembered the hole in the wire had been and experimented with a few dates on the dials. He cheered when the hum locked, but found himself striding out across the rec with a tall, spotty boy.

" 'Ere, Gerry," he's saying to me, "lend us a quid, will yer?" I'm Nick's brother! No thanks — don't want to get into the head of that psycho. I know — Sime's birthday — we came on his birthday once – it's exactly a week after mine. It's a switch! Here I go . . .

Climbing through the wire – I think I must be Sime. Someone's behind me – yeah, it's me, Nathan, eight-year-old prototype. Banging on the door with our secret knock.

"Hurry up! It's bucketing down out here!" Sime's yelling.

"What's the password?" Nick calls.

I turn. "What's the password, Nathe?"

"Just let us in, willya?" this skinny little Nathe yells back, giving the door a kick.

"No, that's not it. You're not coming in till you say it!"

"Hippopotamus!" yells Sime.

"That was last week's!" yells Nick.

We're both kicking the door now. "Come on, Nick – you know it's us!"

"You could be aliens!" he yells back.

He's looking at us through the window.

"It's us – you can see it's us!" we yell.

"Aliens can do that!" he yells back. "They can take over your bodies."

Yeah – that was a laugh, thought Nathan later as he lay on the sofa. Apart from getting soaked through. And the freezing cold. And the boring bits. And Nick's brother. And the smell. And the spiders. Apart from that.

"The doctor thinks it might be some sort of virus," Mum

156

was telling Nan. "Lots of it about, he says. Can last for weeks. Could be up one day and down the next."

"He does look peaky," said Nan.

Mum had taken time off work to take him to the doctor. Nathan had fallen asleep again at school. He sat in the armchair letting the words drift past him. The walk to the surgery and back to Nan's had left him limp.

"Doctor says let him rest – plenty of liquids. Can go back to school when he feels up to it. Anyway, I better get back. Bye, Nathe."

She gave him a kiss and left.

"That's right," said Nan. "you go to sleep."

"I'm OK, Mum," said Nathan a few days later, as he set off for school. But he detoured into Bakery Lane, then into Albert Road and towards Bryjan. He wore the key on a string around his neck these days. He couldn't risk losing it. He broke into a jog, eager to get switching. He'd started to keep a notebook, two columns headed GOOD SWITCHES and BAD SWITCHES, with dates for setting the dials – or avoiding. But he needed to find some new good switches. He'd switched into the same old birthdays and Christmases so many times that the buzzes he got from them were growing weak, as if they'd been watered down. And he couldn't help bumping into the bad switches now and again. All those rows. He'd forgotten about all those rows. And things he didn't want to hear. Things Mum had said to Dad and Dad to Mum, that would send him plummeting downwards.

What did Mr Onslow call it? Empathy – putting yourself in someone else's place. Well, I've had enough empathy. I've got empathy coming out of my ears. All that anger – all that hurt – I don't want everyone else's.

It was like the Saxons and the Normans all over again. One side against the other. What seemed right at the time depended on who you were. Till you changed sides. It was very confusing. One minute he'd be feeling sorry for Mum, and the next for Dad.

And all those rows about me: the broken window, the lost football boots, the stolen bike. Perhaps it was all my fault – Mum leaving. What about that switchback last week – that huge row about my trainers?

"How much? How much?" says Dad. And as I've switched into Dad, I can tell you I'm pretty shocked.

"I'm not paying that for a pair of plimsolls," he says.

"They're trainers, not plimsolls," says Mum, "and if you think you can do better, then you trail round the shops with him."

"I can't believe it's that difficult to buy a decent pair of sensible shoes for half that price," says Dad, "and I'm just not coughing up that sort of money for this rubbish."

"Right!" says Mum, pulling them off my feet and throwing them at him. "Take them back – you're in charge."

"Don't take it out on Nathan," Dad says, because I'm sitting here looking pretty fed up having Mum snatch them off my feet as if it's all my fault – I've only come into the kitchen for a biscuit – and I know if Dad takes me to the shops it'll be the sort of stuff he wears – beige Hush Puppies or something.

"Well – you'd better get a move on. The shops shut in half an hour and we're going on holiday tomorrow. What's he going to wear – wellingtons?" shouts Mum.

"Come on, Nathan. Let's leave her to calm down, shall we?" says Dad. "Come and give us a hand with sweeping the path."

Now whose fault was that? Eh?

". . . so he said – you would if your bum was on fire!"

Nina and Tansy screeched with laughter. Gav looked pleased with himself and his joke.

"Come on, Nathe," nudged Nina, "don't you get it?"

They were in the playground.

"I've heard it before," said Nathan, who hadn't been listening.

He shuffled from foot to foot with restless impatience. They were looking at him.

"You're twitching again," said Gav.

"It's this bug I've got," said Nathan.

"I hope it's not catching," said Tansy. "You ought to go home."

"Looks like you've got bees in your boxers," said Gav.

"Or his bum's on fire!" laughed Tansy.

More guffaws.

"What are we going to do tomorrow, then," said Nina.

"Tomorrow?" said Nathan.

"Yeah – you know – it's an INSET day – a day off – no school."

"What's on at the pictures?" said Tansy.

"We could get a video."

"Boring."

"Tenpin bowling."

"I hate bowling – I'm useless."

"That's decided then," said Nina after exhausting the list of things to do. "OK with everyone?"

"What?" said Nathan. "What's decided?"

"Swimming at the Oasis – what's the matter with you?" said Gav.

"Nah, I don't think I'll bother. I gotta . . ."

"Aw, come on, Nathe! Don't spoil things. It's better with four," said Nina.

"Come on, Nathe!"

"All right."

"Meet up at the bus station at nine-thirty," said Nina.

15

~

All in All, It's Just Another Way Up the Wall

~

Just one more switchback – then I'll stop. Getting fed up with all the old repeats though – need some new switches.

Nathan climbed the stairs to his room, stood by the bed, set the dials and pressed the button.

Not again – Mum making the bed. Dead boring. Lots of the Mum switchbacks are boring.

He flopped onto the chair, idly made a few careless adjustments to the dials and jabbed the button.

Here's something! I'm switching – off I go. It's dark in here – but there's a dim light – a lamp, I think. Who am I? I think I'm wearing a nightie – and fluffy slippers – oh heck – oh heck – I've got – I've got – bosoms. And something's attached to one of them – it's that ugly little baby again. It's me – baby Nathe. And I'm Mum again – in my nightie – looking down at Nathe, the little red-faced gnome. And I'm thinking – Mum's thinking – I can't believe this – she's thinking he's the most beautiful thing in the world – and she touches his fist with a finger and he's grasping it like he's never going to let go. It's that soppy gooey feeling again, only different. It's like she's been injected with something – like liquid sunshine – warm and soft – flushing through her veins – and nothing else matters. And she can't stop looking – and touching. The

161

tiny fingers — the tufty orange — sorry, Titian — hair. He's let go now and he's making all those stupid faces — and Mum's laughing. Someone else is laughing too — it's Dad — behind her, reaching out to touch the gnome's fist. Now he's picking it up, pacing up and down in his pyjamas while the gnome's making this horrible noise. He's starting to sing to it — it's terrible. *"Rock a bye baby"*, he's singing — but it's working — little Nathe the Gnome is nodding off.

Nathan lay on his bed staring up at the ceiling.

Wow. That was something. Twenty out of ten. That was me. That was how Mum and Dad felt about me. All that warm, soft, soppy stuff. All for me. That's the best switch ever.

He closed his eyes. His head was light and woozy. The bed seemed to disappear beneath him and he floated blissfully upwards. He was drifting contentedly when the doorbell rang, causing him to crash land.

Ignore it, Nathe. It'll go away.

Now there was a hammering coming from the back door below his window. He sat up and peered down. Someone stared back at him. It was Nina and she was shouting something. He beamed her a contented, puzzled smile. She glared back and pointed to the door.

"What?" he smiled, opening the window and leaning out.

"Thanks a lot, Nathan Beazer!" she yelled.

What's she thanking me for?

His mind groped dreamily for what he might have given her.

"Well — are you going to let me in or not?" she shouted up.

She charged past him as he opened the door and then turned on him.

"I've been looking everywhere for you! What happened?"

She stood, hands on hips, waiting for an answer.

He shrugged helplessly, beaming his woozy smile.

"What you grinning like that for? You look like an escaped lunatic. Well — I'm waiting!" she demanded. "I want an answer."

"What's the question again?" he asked.

"Where have you been!"

"I've been here — here's where I've been — been here. What's up? What's the hassle?"

"You were supposed to be at the bus station — remember? Nine-thirty? The Oasis? Swimming?"

"Aaaaah." He grinned as the memory slowly resurfaced.

"Is that all you've got to say?" said Nina.

"What would you say," said Nathan slowly, almost giggling at the brilliance of the excuse slowly seeping into his mind, "what would you say if I told you — I'd been kidnapped by aliens and taken to the planet Zarpong and the last ten hours are a complete mystery to me?"

"I'd say it's a pity they bothered to bring you back!"

She folded her arms and stared at the taps.

"It's not funny, Nathe. We waited for over an hour. Gav and Tansy got fed up and went on without me. I've been to your mum's – your nan's – I came here once but there was no answer. Then I came back again and saw your bag in the kitchen, through the window. I was really looking forward to it, Nathe. Today's been a complete waste – thanks to you."

What's the hurry? What's the worry? said his brain.

"We can still go," he suggested cheerily. "Yeah – let's go, Nina. I'll dive from the top board – always wanted to do that – a double backflip – come on – let's go."

She looked at him sideways.

"It's too late now. I've got to pick up my little sister soon."

She flopped onto a chair and drew patterns with her finger on the kitchen table.

"Whose is that?" she asked, pointing to the guitar leaning against the wall.

"My dad's."

"You didn't tell me he played."

"He doesn't."

"Can I have a look?"

"Help yourself."

He watched her balance it on her knee, position her fingers and strum.

"Needs tuning a bit – that's better."

Then she was playing. Humming a tune as she strummed and her fingers stepped up and down the frets.

"Hey – that's great," he smiled.

"It's blues," she informed him. "It's not hard – you have

a go. Put your fingers like this – no, move that finger – go on – now run your other thumb down the strings."

Yeah – it is easy, dead easy. Everything's easy.

"I could get to like this," he said. "Go on – show us some more – another chord."

She looked at her watch.

"I ought to be going. Look – come back with me. Bring the guitar. I've got loads of books and chord charts – you can borrow them if you like. I'll teach you – come on."

He thrust the guitar back into its case and grabbed his bag, following her out. *You've left the switch on your bed*, Nathe, a little voice reminded him.

"Hold on," he called, halfway down the path. "I've forgotten something."

He reached for the key around his neck. Where was it? He peered down his T-shirt.

It's not there. Where is it? Must have lifted it off with the switch – it's still inside – with the switch – got to get them back.

He ran round through the carport into the back garden.

No problem. It's OK, he told himself. My window's still open – I can get in through the window. Easy-peasy. Relax.

"Can't it wait, Nathe?" said Nina, following.

"I'll only be a sec," he said, tossing down his bag and pulling himself up onto the window ledge. He reached for the drainpipe.

"Are you sure you know what you're doing, Nathe?"

She watched him get a foothold on the drainpipe bracket.

"*All in all – it's just another way up the wall,*" he sang.

"It's a synch!" he called, reaching up for a grip on the trellis behind the creeper.

"Be careful, Nathe. What if you fall?"

Then I'll fly, he grinned to himself. Nearly there now.

There was a ripping sound as the trellis came away from the wall. Then a sharp crack. Then he *was* flying. Backwards. Till something hit him. Hard. In the back. He felt like a swatted fly. He saw dancing lights, heard a swooping hum.

"Switch off – switch off," he mumbled.

Now he was floating upwards, looking down at himself lying spreadeagled on the ground and Nina kneeling over him.

"Told you I could fly." He laughed.

But she didn't seem to hear. He saw her jump up and run. There was a sudden whoosh and he plummeted downwards into a smothering darkness.

166

16
~
Not Just Another Brick in the Wall
~

Leave me alone! Leave me alone!

Hands were tugging at him.

Fingers were poking him.

Now wrenching his eyes open.

A blinding light. Dazzling. White, gold and red; hot.

Don't poke my eyes out! Please! I wasn't in the forest – nowhere near it! It wasn't me – honest!

Voices. Echoing voices.

"Nathan! Nathan! Can you hear me – hear me – hear me-me-me ee-ee-ee . . ."

It echoed and faded.

"Switch off," he whimpered.

He opened his eyes.

Mum? Dad? Nan? They look terrible – what's the matter with them?

Now suddenly they were smiling, beaming at him.

"Nathe?" cried Mum, leaning over him.

Dad leapt to his feet, cried, "Nurse!" and disappeared behind a horrible green curtain covered in purple and orange flowers.

"Thank God," said Mum.

"Hello, Mum. Hello, Nan," he said. "Was Dad here or did I dream it?"

As Dad reappeared, it all came back to him, like a slide show before his eyes. The guitar – *You're pathetic, Dad* – Nina – climbing the wall – falling – *You're pathetic, Dad*...

"I'm sorry, Dad," he said.

"You're sorry? No, Nathe, it's me who should be sorry. Your nan told me – about the guitar – all the trouble you went to – and I'd like to say thanks. It – well, it made me think. Now you just get better, eh?"

"Yes, Nathe," Mum said, stroking his hand, "that's all that matters."

He could see Nan at the end of the bed, dabbing her eyes.

"Where's Nina?" asked Nathan.

"She had to go home," said Mum. "I'll let her know you're all right – she was very worried. Thank heavens she was there."

Now a nurse was bending over him, lifting his eyelids, examining his pulse.

"Hello there. How are you feeling now? Can you tell me your name?"

What a stupid question.

"Nathan Beazer."

Everyone smiled and nodded as if it was the cleverest thing they'd ever heard. His name didn't usually have this effect.

"His reflexes are back to normal," said the nurse, "and

the X-rays show no damage, but the doctor will want to examine him properly. He'll have to stay here for at least twenty-four hours. We have to be careful with concussion cases. Try and keep him talking. Best if he doesn't fall asleep again."

But he did. Before his eyelids drooped he saw Mum and Dad sitting either side of him, and Nan beside Dad. All together again. Just like it used to be.

Excellent, Nathe. Nathan the Invincible.

He stayed in hospital for two weeks.

"Curious. Very curious," said Dr Latimer. "He hasn't been in the tropics lately, has he?"

Dr Latimer was concerned about the heavy sleeping, and the confusion that followed. Not to mention the twitching. Nina visited every day. Mike brought him a huge box of chocolates and Gav called by and helped him eat them. Slowly he returned to his old self.

That was close, Nathe. The switch had you hooked. You gotta stay off it, Nathe. A switchaholic – that's what you were. A switchaholic, he told himself, as Dad drove them to Mum's flat.

They sat, drinking cups of tea and eating custard creams. Mum looked different; smart in her grey suit and sleek hair. Dad was different too; more like the old Dad in the switch-backs.

"We want to talk to you, Nathe," said Mum.

"Sort things out a bit," said Dad. "Your Mum and me – we've been discussing the future."

Mum was discussing the future? With Dad? Nathan sat up.

"And what we've agreed . . ." said Mum.

Agree? They've actually agreed? You've done it, Nathe! You've done it!

". . . is to divorce," said Dad.

Nathan slumped.

It's all your own fault, Nathe. You were the one who told Dad she was never coming back. Things might have been OK if you'd kept your mouth shut. Nathan the Bigmouth.

"We're going to sell the house," said Dad.

"What? Sell Bryjan?" he blurted.

"Don't call it that — I always hated that stupid name," said Mum.

"Well, thank you very much — now you tell me — hours of work went into that," said Dad.

"I liked it," said Nathan.

"Anyway," said Dad, "I'll find a smaller place — with room for you of course . . ."

"And I'll start looking for a bigger place — with plenty of room for you, Nathe . . ."

"And you'll be with your mother when she's at home . . ."

"And at your father's when I'm away," said Mum.

"The most important thing . . ." Dad said.

". . . is you," said Mum.

"To both of us," said Dad.

He stood up.

"So — I'll be seeing you soon, eh, Nathan? And don't go climbing any more walls. Oh yes — nearly forgot. Here's your key. Found it on the bed with that old box. Can't work out what that is at all. Like to take it apart and have a good look sometime. Bit busy at the moment."

Next day, straight after school, Nathan hurried to Dad's. The switch was on his bed. He examined it carefully for signs of tampering and breathed a sigh of relief to find it still intact.

I'll decide what to do with you later, he told it, wrapping it in a pair of pyjama trousers. You're too valuable – and dangerous – to be left lying around.

"Home, home on the range," sang Nathan as he strummed his guitar.

He'd mastered a number of chords now and several strumming rhythms, and joined Nina and the others in Miss Dickenson's Friday guitar lessons. And at lunch times a few of them got together to practise.

There was a triple ring at the front doorbell of the flat. He put down his guitar, went to the window and waved down to Dad to let him know he was on his way. Dad was taking him and Nina swimming at the Oasis. He decided not to attempt the double backflip. He could just about manage the low diving board. He hated heights. Always had. Just the thought of climbing that wall gave him the jitters.

How'd I do that? Spooky.

Dad bought a Chinese takeaway on the way back. The BRYJAN nameplate had gone from the gate. And the FOR

SALE sign had a red and white stripe announcing SOLD across it. As Nathan fetched some plates from the cupboard, he noticed a pile of faded coloured papers on the worktop. Some covered in daubs of paint, an ancient seed picture consisting of a few sorry-looking lentils and dried peas, a calendar made from an old birthday card and a grubby, greasy, brick-shaped piece of card covered in brownish splodges of paint.

"Found those behind the fridge when I was clearing up," said Dad.

Nathan turned the brick-shaped card over. **Nathan** was scrawled in thick black crayon on the back and below it were three peeling gold stars.

Is this it? Is this the amazing brick I was so proud of? Three stars for this? It's rubbish. Miss King must have been mad.

He stuffed it into the kitchen bin.

"Nearly forgot," said Dad as he dropped Nathan off outside Mum's flat. He reached into his pocket for an envelope.

"I'm helping out at the Players Theatre – making the scenery and props – backstage stuff for the drama club at work. Got a couple of free tickets for the play next week. Your nan's going – why don't you come along – bring Nina too."

"Thanks, Dad."

I've gotta tell someone, thought Nathan as he ambled to school. Soon. Who though? The police? MI5? The Prime

Minister? Who's in charge of time switches, exactly? The sort of time switch that switches you into other people and into the past. And who's gonna believe me? They're gonna take a lot of convincing.

The problem pressed down on him. He couldn't shrug it off. The switch lay wrapped in his pyjamas at the back of a drawer but he could sense its silent presence and imagine its humming.

I can't just leave it there, can I? And sometimes, sometimes I think — just one more go. I mean — there's so much more I could do with it. What about old Hamish McKay? I'd love to find out about him. If I could sneak into Glebe House and switch back, I'm sure I'd find some clues. But what if the switch got into the wrong hands? Just think about that, Nathe. This could be big trouble — too big for you to handle.

I know someone I'd like to show it to, though. Mr Onslow.

Nathan had grown to like Mr Onslow. He'd taken a keen interest in Nathan. Relieved him from the boredom of those lonely vigils in Mrs Sanderson's office while on report by supervising him in the history room, word-processing his Saxon experience, expressing a delight in Nathan's expert knowledge.

Just think — I could take him to the castle — show him what it was like to be a Norman knight — watch the castle grow. Yeah — I'd love to see his face when I show him all that. I mean — just a bit of old wall and he's going on about it as if he's discovered a new planet. What if I got him switching back to see the walls going up? The Normans and Saxons right before his eyes. But I'd have to warn him, wouldn't I? The dangers – the side effects. Yeah – I'll show the switch to him first. There might not be a chance later. Not when the Prime Minister gets to hear about it. And the Queen probably. Maybe President Clinton even. They'll probably confiscate it – for reasons of national security.

Boy! This thing is going to be big! And what about me? What'll happen to me? I'll ask Mr Onslow. He'll know what to do. I'll swear him to secrecy first. It must be worth millions, this switch. I'll buy an electric guitar. Black. And a white one for Nina. A new car for Dad. A house for Mum. What about Nan? A lifetime's supply of gingernuts. And that lampshade she wanted. An all-expenses-paid trip to Australia to buy one.

He turned into Bakery Lane. And stopped. The wall – *his* wall – had gone. Most of it, anyway. And the bakery. Only the church hall, or part of it, was still standing.

He wandered over and stood staring at the man in the yellow helmet busy chipping away at the wall that remained.

"Magenta," said Nathan.

"You say something?" said the man, straightening up.

"Magenta – that's what that red-purply colour's called."

He pointed to a brick.

"Well – you might have something there," said the man, lifting his helmet and wiping away the sweat with the back of his hand. He bent and lifted the brick from a neatly stacked pile.

"See this," he said. "This is what they call a Luton Purple."

"No kidding?" said Nathan.

"Though how they got to be in these walls – well – that's a bit of a mystery. You don't get Luton Purples round these parts. Must have been brought in specially. There were lines of them running all along the wall, every eighth row. This wasn't just any old wall, you know."

"I could tell," said Nathan. "Seems a real shame, knocking it down. I liked that wall. Gonna be dumped are they?"

"Dumped? Not these. I've bought this lot – taking them back to my yard. Reclaimed, these are. They'll be used again. Repairing walls, rebuilding – quite a demand these days. Good old bricks these – hand made. Look," he said, turning the brick over, "see these lines?"

He ran his finger along a sweep of shallow, curving, parallel lines.

"This brick was made by pressing clay into a mould – these are drag lines made by the wire that cut the clay level – a wire stretched on a bow. A machine would have left straight lines. And – ah – now here's something. See this?"

He pointed to an indentation on the side of the brick.

"Know what that is?"

Nathan shook his head.

"That's a thumb print – from whoever made this brick when it was soft clay – over two hundred years ago, I'd say. Now there's history for you."

"Yeah – it is! It's a thumb print – I can see it," said

Nathan with excitement. "It's amazing — a two-hundred-year-old thumb print. I know someone who'd find this really interesting."

"Here you are, then," said the man. "You show them."

"What? I can have it?"

"I can spare it — got thousands here. Especially to someone who recognises a good brick when he sees one."

"Cor! Thanks."

And hugging his brick, he set off again for school.

All in all it's *not* just another brick in the wall.

17

~

Switching Over

~

"*A Midsummer Night's Dream* – by William Shakespeare,"
said Nan, reading the theatre programme.

"You all right there, Nina? Oh – look, Nathan – your
dad's name's in it. Backstage – Phil Hunt, Diane Fetcher
and Bryan Beazer."

Nathan, Nan and Nina sat in the seats of the little
Players Theatre, watching people searching for their seats
and squeezing past those already seated, who crouched
awkwardly to let them through.

"Just fancy," said Nan. "I never thought it'd be this
busy."

"Dad said he'd come and say hello before the start," said
Nathan, craning his neck.

"Well – he's left it too late," said Nan. "Look – the
lights are going down."

A hush fell as the curtains opened.

A group of people wearing what looked like nightdresses
stood on stage.

"Now, fair Hippolyta, our nuptial hour draws on apace,"
said one of the actors.

Nathan sighed and slid down into his seat. As the play
progressed it became clear that nuptials featured heavily in
this play. He'd worked out by now it was just another word
for wedding. There were lots of methinks, and betwixts, and

talk of merriments. No decent sword fights, ghosts or blood. Nothing worth coming for at all. He squinted down at the programme.

Leaping doodahs. *This play lasts approximately three hours,* he read. *There will be an interval of twenty minutes.* He could only hope that it was a misprint and that it was meant the other way round.

The man next to him started chuckling. Nathan stared up at him with curiosity and then back to the stage. It was a different group on stage now; workmen wearing overalls and flat caps. The whole audience was laughing. It seemed that the workmen were planning to put on a play for one of the weddings. One of the workmen was called Bottom. Nick Bottom.

Give me Tissue-head any day, thought Nathan. Imagine what it'd be like at school with a name like Nick Bottom. Life wouldn't be worth living. The others had odd names too. Quince and Snout and Snug and Flute and Starveling.

Now they were in the wood with the Fairies. Bottom had been changed into a donkey by a spell and the Queen of the Fairies, under another spell, had fallen in love with him, stroking his furry ears and calling him her angel. Then Bottom was himself again and they were in the woods getting ready to perform their play for the wedding. Suddenly a piece of the scenery walked forward. It was a wall wearing a bushy beard, a flat cap and wellingtons. Snout, in fact, acting the part of the wall, wearing a large board painted with bricks, suspended by straps over his shoulders.

"Oi, one Snout boi nay-m, pree-sent a worl," he announced slowly.

Nathan leaned forward. Snout looked oddly familiar beneath his bushy beard and his flat cap and his folksy drawl.

"An' such ay worl as oi would 'ave you think
tha' 'ad innit – a crannied 'ole – or chink . . ."

Snout made a circle with his finger and thumb with one hand and waggled the fingers of his other hand through the circle to show the hole. The audience laughed.

". . . through which – the lovers, Pyramus and Thisbe
did whisper often – very secret-lee . . ."

It's Dad! thought Nathan. I'm sure it is. Snout is Dad.

"Hey, Nan! Nina! Look – it's Dad. It's Dad!"

"Well, I'll be—" said Nan. "So it is."

Snout is Dad, thought Nathan. And he's playing a wall! A bloomin' wall!

Now the two lovers in the play were trying to talk and kiss through the chink in the wall that separated them. Only Snout, absent-mindedly, swung the wall board that was strapped to his shoulders, sending one of them sprawling. The audience roared. It was more like a pantomime than a play. As she found her feet, the other lover disappeared behind the wall. Snout leaned over to help him up and sent the other flying again. The audience were roaring with laughter. Nan had tears streaming down her face.

"An' bein' dun – thus worl ay-way doth go," said Snout, as eventually the lovers finished the scene and limped off.

There was huge applause as, crab-like, Snout, with the wide wall swinging, edged to the side of the stage. He struggled for several seconds trying to manoeuvre the wall through, gave up and tiptoed back on stage, searching for another exit. Aiming at a narrow space between two bushes he crashed and rebounded backwards. The audience roared as they watched him make several attempts to get up again. Nathan's ribs hurt from laughing. Now Snout was groping for a way out through the curtains, disappearing for a few seconds while they watched him stumble his way behind, only to wander out again, scratching his head, and looking lost. At each attempt the audience cheered and clapped. Till finally Snug, dressed as the lion in the play, came on and dragged him off sideways.

"More! More!" cried a man in the back row as the audience cheered and clapped. Nathan clapped till his hands tingled.

Charisma, Dad. Charisma.

"I didn't know your dad was in it," said Nina. "He was brilliant."

"Well – fancy that," said Nan.

They had trouble finding Dad backstage. It was crowded and Dad was surrounded by people. He saw them and beckoned them over.

"You were amazing, Dad," said Nathan. "You're the best wall I've ever seen."

"Brilliant," said Nina.

"That's right – you tell him," interrupted the Queen of the Fairies. "You know, your dad only had a few hours' notice. Our other wall went down with appendicitis at half past three. Word perfect he was too, your dad."

"Just a good memory, that's all," said Dad. "Anyway – picked it up from watching the rehearsals. Nerve-racking though – I think I'll stick with making scenery in the future."

"No chance – not after that performance," said Bottom.

"Any more to come, Nathe?" said Mum as Nathan crammed the binbag full of clothes into the back of the van.

"A couple of boxes, I think."

"Where's it all come from?" said Mum. "I didn't have this much stuff when I moved in."

They were moving to a larger flat that Mum had found. Mike had borrowed a van for the day and Nina was helping too.

"Where do you want this?" said Nina's voice from behind a walking laundry basket.

There was a shout from above. Mike was at the window with a box in his arms.

"I think this is the last," he yelled, "but you better come and check!"

"Coming!" yelled Mum, running back in.

As Mike stepped back, Nathan saw something tip from the window. It unfolded like a huge bird and, as if in slow motion, his pyjama bottoms wafted gently down, the legs like crumpled wings, releasing something from their folds: a box, wooden, the size of a thick book. It dropped like a brick. He heard its sickening crash almost before it flashed before his eyes and disappeared into the stairwell of the basement flat.

"No!" he heard someone scream.

It was him.

He surged forward and ran down the steps as his pyjamas floated softly down on top of the splintered wood, as if it was the decent thing to do, like covering a corpse with a sheet.

Nathan felt a pain in his chest. A real pain. Not imagined. The pain of something lost, never to be recovered. Something lost for ever.

He pushed aside the pyjamas and forced himself to look. For one millisecond, when he saw that the clasps of the lid were still in position, he felt a spark of hope, but as he picked it up, the sides and bottom fractured and fell apart. Coils of wire disgorged like lifeless snakes. A dial fell and rolled drunkenly into a pile of rubbish. From the depths of the crushed box, something flickered. He stared. A pyramid-shaped crystal, like a shard of blue ice, pulsed weakly. As Nathan carefully lifted it, it broke, shattering into pieces that faded and dimmed, till his hand held nothing more than broken chunks of dull greyish stone. He crouched, staring.

Nina, who had caught up with him, stood on the steps behind, leaning forward.

"Lucky it didn't hit someone," she said. "Looks wrecked. What is it? Not worth anything, is it?"

"Only about several million pounds," groaned Nathan.

The two guitars, Dad's new car, Mum's new house and Nan's gingernuts shimmered before his eyes like pale ghosts, fizzed and vanished with a pop.

"You're kidding," laughed Nina. "That old thing? Anyway – I've seen it before. It was in your schoolbag. I saw it when I had to take it to the office after you went mental that time in maths."

"Nina," said Nathan. "This is not just any old box. You've heard of time machines, haven't you? Well – this is a time *switch* – it'll switch you into the past – into another person in the past. Look – here's the switch."

He waggled the loose switch; it came away in his fingers.

"And here's a time dial."

He crouched down to pick up the dial.

"Get away, Nathe." She grinned. "Why can't you ever be serious?"

"I am serious," he said. "How do you think I did my 'Day in the Life of a Saxon' story, eh?"

"Shut up, Nathe. You're really weird sometimes, you know."

Slowly he stood up. And as he straightened, it was as if he was shedding a great heaviness, making him remember the time he'd switched back into the Norman knight. How, when his two young squires had helped him from his horse and lifted the tunic of heavy chain mail from his shoulders, he had felt that same lightness of body that he felt now. A feeling of floating freedom. Had Hamish McKay known that feeling too? Had he deliberately abandoned the switch?

I don't think the world was ready for you yet, thought Nathan, as he gathered the pieces together on the pyjamas.

Shame about old Onslow, though. He was chuffed to bits

with that brick, especially when I let him keep it. I'd really have loved to have shown him how to switch.

Mike leant over the basement rails.

"Sorry, mate!" he called down. "I'll buy you another one, whatever it was. Don't know how it happened – really stupid. Real sorry, like. Could kick myself."

"Don't worry about it. No one's perfect," said Nathan.

He rolled the bundle under his arm and slipped the chunks of stone into his pocket.

"Nathe! Nina? Are you ready?" called Mum. "Everything's packed and ready to go."

Yep, thought Nathan as they climbed into the van, I'm ready. Nathan the Ready. Ready for anything.

"Only two more weeks and it's the holidays," said Nina, as Mum started the van.

"Is it?" said Nathan.

Great – I'm really looking forward to the holidays, he decided. A good word: holidays. Summer holidays – even better. Sunshine yellow, sky blue, grass green, aquamarine, cherry, strawberry, nectarine . . .

Inside his pocket his hand stroked the largest chunk of stone.

"Here, Neen, can you smell strawberries?"

"I can smell this binbag I'm shoved up against," said Nina.

"But it's really strong," said Nathan, "go on – you must be able to smell it."

As his fingers rubbed the stone the taste of strawberries filled his mouth. And against his palm that held the stone, he felt a pulsing warmth. He withdrew his fist and opened it. In the dim light of the van the stone turned opaque; shimmered. A tiny, luminous crystal of light, like an eye which seemed to wink at him.

Also by Pat Moon

THE SPYING GAME

Shortlisted for the Guardian Children's Fiction Award 1994
Shortlisted for the Best Children's Book Category of
Writers' Guild Awards 1994

Why should the man who killed Joe's father still be walking around as if nothing had happened? Could it have been an accident after all?

Loathing and anger build up so much inside Joe that he begins a secret, carefully planned persecution of the man and his family. A scratch down the side of his new car, anonymous hate mail, graffiti: nothing too desperate, but just enough for the man to know that someone is watching him – all the time.

"A stunningly powerful novel which grips the reader – truly engrossing."   BOOKS FOR YOUR CHILDREN

DOUBLE IMAGE

Shortlisted for the Smarties Book Prize 1993

A faded photograph of a boy who could be David's double. An old suitcase full of books, papers and photographs. A completely empty bedroom shut off at the top of the house. David's grandfather hides a secret which no one will talk about and which has lain buried for many years.

Slowly David pieces together all the clues. And, as he discovers the identity of the other boy, a gripping story unfolds.

"The unfolding mystery kept me turning the pages."
                                              BOOKS FOR KEEPS